Saving All My Love for You

A young lovers story penned by:

B. Love

www.authorblove.com

Author Page - www.facebook.com/authorblove
Instagram – www.instagram.com/authorblove
Twitter – www.twitter.com/authorblove
Website – www.authorblove.com
Paperback books – www.blovesbooks.com
Self-love   classes!   -   http://blove.teachable.com

Harlem was like... an egg.

Hard exterior that was meant to protect the softness that was inside, but that hard exterior was way too fragile and easily cracked. She needed to be handled carefully. I understood that. Knight understood that. But Carmen and Princeton... even Tage... they couldn't. Yes, she was outspoken and seemingly rebellious and uncaring, but at the end of the day... she was a little girl. A little girl with a big belly and big responsibility.

She was an egg.

Hard. Fragile. Soft.

— Charlie White–Carver

HARLEM

Being with Tage left me in ruins. Hayden, our two-year-old son made those ruins beautiful, but Tage ruined me. Not in that typical romantic sexy way. Where the man makes it impossible for any other man to be with the woman. No. I mean Tage *ruined* me. Destroyed my soul. Left my heart broken and open... love for him seeping out... only to decay.

Woah.

That's way too deep and depressing.

Especially as I sit here and watch our son gobble up the ice cream that his auntie Charlie knows good and damn well I told her he couldn't have! But Hayden was like Tage in that way. He had this... unspoken charm that would cause you to fold and give him just about anything he could ever ask you for.

So let me start from the beginning.

I met Tage my freshman year of high school. He was a sophomore and far more familiar with the school and classes than I was. With no idea of which direction to go, there I was – standing in the middle of the hall frozen while everyone around me made their way to where they needed to be. When Tage first approached me my head was down as I looked at my schedule, so I didn't see anything but his feet at the sound of his voice.

He asked me what class I was trying to find, and at the sound of his voice my eyes closed. My heart fluttered. My body shivered. No, it wasn't because his voice was like that of a god. It wasn't all deep or melodious or smooth. It wasn't so much how his voice sounded but how his voice made me feel. Then I looked up and into his eyes and fell hopelessly in puppy love and lust with his fine ass!

After staring so long my mouth moistened, Tage took my schedule from my hand with a smile and looked it over. He nodded and grabbed my hand, then led me to my class. I still hadn't said anything to him by the time we made it to the door. Tage handed me my schedule back and that was that. He turned and left and the spell he had me under was broken.

It was then that I realized how stupid and immature I must've looked, but I couldn't help it. Tage was the most beautiful boy I'd ever seen. The sight of him literally made me speechless. I spent my entire time in class daydreaming about him. It wasn't until the bell rang and we were dismissed that I was pulled back into reality.

I made my way outside, and to my surprise… Tage was standing at the door. Waiting. For me. He walked me to my next class. And the next. And the next. That became our thing. He'd meet me at the same place every day and walk me to all of my classes. An entire week went by before I was able to finally talk to him… and when I did… that sealed our fate.

My sophomore year I got pregnant and here we are. Well, me and Hayden. This is where we are. Tage is in Alabama.

"All I'm saying is, Charlie and I have more than enough room for you and Hayden. Even with the new baby on the way. You don't have to leave, Harlem. I wanted you to stay at least until you were 21 anyway."

That was my boo. My big brother. Knight Carver. He was my hero. My heart. I moved in with him when I was four months pregnant. Our father, Princeton, told me that I had to get an abortion to stay with him because he wasn't raising anymore kids. Of course I wasn't going to do that, so Knight took me in.

He met his wife Charlie when we went to Bundled. She used to work there. I needed some maternity clothes and things for the baby and Charlie helped us. In more ways than one. They ended up getting married and having Knight Jr. Now Charlie's pregnant with baby number two.

They both do so much for Hayden and I appreciate all they've done for me, but I just feel as if the time has come for me to be on my own. Their family is growing and I don't want to stand in the way of what they have going on. They couldn't even really enjoy their newlywed phase because I was in the house with a newborn baby. Of course they would never say that, but I just don't want us to be in the way anymore. It's time for me and Hayden to go.

"I hear you, boo, and I really appreciate you and Charlie, but it's time to go. I'm 18. I'll be starting college in a few months. My store is doing great thanks to you. It's time, Knight."

After Hayden was born I opened a dropship clothing business. With the help of Charlie, I pulled in twenty thousand my first year open. I did drop shipping for two years, and on my eighteenth birthday Knight bought me a storefront. Now I have my own clothing store – Hayden's Corner.

So at this point it really didn't matter what Knight and Charlie said. They've done so much for me that I just straight up refuse to take any more help from them. Thanks to them I'm doing a lot better than most people twice my age financially. I've got my beautiful yet crazy little boy. My business is doing great and I'll be starting school soon. What more could I ask of them?

"But college isn't like high school, Harlem. I won't be there to wake your ass up and make sure you get to school on time. Charlie won't be there to ask you about homework and projects. It will all be on you. Do you really think you can handle college, the business, bills and cooking and cleaning on top of taking care of Hayden?"

Well, when he said it like that it sounded like a lot. I wouldn't tell him that, though.

"I can do all things through Christ who is my strength, Knight."

"You and Charlie always quoting that scripture when I ask y'all the simplest questions."

I chuckled and stood before answering.

"Where do you think I get it from? I'm going to be fine, Knight. Seriously. If I can't handle it, I know that I can always come back here."

As he talked I walked over to Hayden and squatted to kiss his wet, cold, ice cream covered lips.

"Fine. Let's make a deal. You stay here until the winter. Until Christmas break. Just to give yourself time to get adjusted to school. And if you still want to leave I'll move your stuff out myself."

"Fair enough. Deal," I directed my attention to Hayden who was too busy making a mess with his ice cream to notice I was getting ready to leave. "I love you, baby. I'll see you tonight. Be good, okay?"

Hayden nodded while finally putting his spoon down and looking at me.

"Where you going?"

With a roll of my eyes I stood and went to grab my purse. Knight was always asking me where I was going. Now he had Hayden doing it.

"Work. Is that okay with you?"

Hayden shrugged and nodded again. He returned his attention to his ice cream and started eating again.

"You're not going to tell me you love me back, DenDen?"

"I love you too," he grumbled. Like I was getting on his nerves. I swear between Tage and Knight, Hayden had the spirit of a grumpy, impatient 80-year-old sometimes.

Knight chuckled as he walked me to the door.

"Thanks again for watching him."

"You don't have to thank me for watching my nephew, sweetheart."

Now I was the one nodding while I hugged him.

"I know, but thanks anyway."

I rushed out of the door before Knight could say anything else. Really I didn't have to go to the store every day, but I chose to. It was my way of getting out of the house and having a break. By the time I finished dealing with employees, customers, payroll, shipments and inventory on top of promotion and marketing it never really was a break, but whatever. It was a break from being in the house and I needed that.

Before Hayden I was hardly ever at home. After Hayden I became a homebody. The store was my way of getting out without feeling guilty about being away from my son. It wasn't like I was hanging with friends or clubbing or no shit like that. I hardly hung out with my best friend anymore. Princess was my ace, but after I had Hayden… I didn't want to do anything but stay home and lay up with him.

For the first year Princess was very understanding of that. She would always come over and kick it with us. I would go out with her maybe once every two months or so. Eventually she got to the point where she stopped trying to hang with me and I completely understand that. This was her time to be wild and free, not cooped up in the house kicking it with me and my DenDen.

Every blue moon she stopped by or we'd go out. Sometimes she'd stop by the store. But for the most part we only talked at school. Now with it being summer break I wasn't expecting to see her for a while.

Every day, though, she FaceTimed Hayden after I got home and got him settled. I was sure we'd always be best friends. Just… best friends traveling down two completely different paths. All I could do was pray that she wised up and saw what that path got me and slowed her hot ass down.

I was almost at the store when I got a call from Tage. Just the sight of his name on my phone had me rolling my eyes. It's crazy how you could hate someone just as much as you used to love them. I started to not answer. He couldn't talk to Hayden since I wasn't around him, and I most definitely didn't want to talk to him. I found myself putting his call on the Bluetooth in my car and answering anyway.

"Hello?"

"Hey, what's up?"

I rolled my eyes again as my grip on the steering wheel tightened. Hating Tage wasn't something I wanted to do… to feel. If anything, hating him came from not being able to really love him.

"What's up?"

"I'm coming home. I'll be there tomorrow."

"Cool. I'll take Hayden to your house in the morning."

"Thanks, Harlem."

Before I had Hayden, Tage had the hardest time telling his parents that I was pregnant. When he finally told them his father made it perfectly clear that he didn't want Hayden to ruin Tage's future and chance of being in the NFL. Between my brother and Tage's brother it seemed like they were able to talk some sense into Tage. He promised he'd be there for me and the baby.

He wasn't.

Tage didn't start seeing Hayden until he was six months old.

It wasn't until Hayden was one that Tage starting seeing him consistently. He'd come back to Memphis every weekend to spend time with Hayden. Because I didn't want to see him I dropped Hayden off with Tage's mother, Patricia. That was hard in itself to do because I couldn't stand Tage's father, but I put up with him for Hayden.

I haven't seen Tage in a little over a year, and to be honest, I don't know how I'd handle seeing him at this point. Tage wasn't just my first love. My high school sweetheart. He was the first person besides Princess that I truly allowed myself to be myself with. He was the first person that I expressed my grief over losing my mother to. He was my best friend. My greatest disappointment and heartache. And every time I think about the fact that he just tossed Hayden and me to the side...

"No problem."

I was about to disconnect the call but his voice stopped me.

"Harlem?"

"Yea?"

He didn't speak right away. Seconds passed before I heard him breathe heavily into the phone.

"Nothing."

"Okay."

Without waiting for him to say more I disconnected the call. Yea, I definitely wouldn't be able to handle seeing him. Not when I could hardly stand hearing his voice.

TAGE

Every time I open my phone and see DenDen and Harlem as my background I feel like shit. There's no excuse I could use to justify leaving them. I could say it was because my pops was adamant about me leaving Memphis and making it big in the NFL, but that would be a pebble in the foundation of the true reason why I left. Yea, my pops was the reason I left, but he wasn't the reason I stayed away.

He wasn't the reason I hardly called and visited. Truth of the matter was, I stayed away because I wasn't ready for the responsibility. I wasn't ready to be a father. I was 17 with my life already planned for me. Having a son wasn't in the plans for another 10 years.

But I met Harlem. I fell in love with her beauty. Her innocence. Her maturity. Her outspoken take no shit attitude. Her sweet heart. I fell in love with her. Made love to her. And out of that love Hayden was conceived.

We had been careful up until that point. That night. Smoking and drinking got the best of us and I went in without a condom. I haven't taken a drink since.

It took me about a year to get into the swing of this whole father thing. I had no problem sending Harlem money, but it took me time to adjust to seeing Hayden and spending time with him. He looked so much like Harlem as a baby. Now he's starting to look like me. Now I can't get enough of him. Hayden is my whole entire world, and I'm finally at a place mentally and emotionally where I'm ready to do all I can to give him the love and life he deserves.

Going from Tuscaloosa to Memphis every weekend to have him is cool, but I've been seriously reconsidering moving back to Memphis to be closer to my son. I didn't want to move to Alabama anyway. That was my father's choice. He said The University of Alabama had one of the best football teams, and my chances of getting in the league would be greater there. Football. That was his choice too.

I love football don't get me wrong, but as far as playing in the NFL is concerned... I could take or leave it. Since a kid football has been my life because it was my father's life. My true passion, though? Flying. Since I flew my first model airplane at five I've wanted to be a pilot. That desire deepened when I started flying real planes at 17. But it was because of my love for my father and desire to please him that I made football my priority and put flying on the backburner.

His reasoning – you can always fly planes. Football is a young man's game.

He'd have a fit if I dropped out and came home and that's the last thing I want now that his drinking has worsened, so this summer the goal is to find a way to please him and my mother while being the father and man I need to be to Hayden and Harlem.

Harlem.

As I sent her a FaceTime request, I dropped the keys to my new apartment on the counter. I signed a lease for a year, but had already told the leasing manager that I might end up paying the two thousand to get out of my lease. I guess it would all depend on how things worked out with Harlem. My furniture wasn't going to be delivered until tomorrow, so all I planned on doing now was bringing my clothes and shit in, then I was going to head to my parents' home to scoop up DenDen.

As always, Harlem accepted the request and handed the phone to Hayden. Every time I FaceTime her she hands the phone to him as soon as she answers. Her petty ass just refuses to let me see her.

Doesn't matter how many times I change phones; I make sure I keep all of the pictures we took. If it wasn't for that and her social media I would never get to see her face, and she hardly ever posts on there anymore.

"What's up, young man?" I spoke to Hayden, and he wasted no time cheesing and showing off practically every tooth in his little mouth.

"Hey, Daddy!"

"Hey, baby boy. What you doing?"

"Reading mommy a bedtime story."

He had the most serious look on his face. I was trying not to laugh but I couldn't help myself.

"But it's morning, DenDen."

Hayden shrugged and pulled the phone closer to his face. His cheeks and mouth took up the entire screen.

"I'll have him at your house in 30 minutes, Tage," Harlem informed me from behind the phone.

"That's cool. I need to talk to you. You think you can wait there for me?"

She was silent. Too silent. I don't know why I even asked her that. I knew she would say no. She wouldn't have been Harlem if she didn't say no.

"I can't, Tage. Just call me later and tell me whatever you have to tell me. Or text it to me. That would be best."

"Whatever, Harlem. Hayden, pull the phone back so I can see your face," Hayden pulled the phone back with a smile. "Turn the phone around so I can see your mama."

"Don't you turn that phone around, Hayden."

We both laughed and shook our head.

"I'll see you in a little while, okay, baby boy?"

Hayden nodded, then dropped the phone and returned to telling Harlem her bedtime story. I listened for a little while before disconnecting the call and heading outside to grab the rest of my things out of the car.

HARLEM

Every Friday I took a walk around the river behind Knight and Charlie's home. When I returned from dropping Hayden off with Patricia, I always put my purse and phone and stuff down, grabbed my iPod, and headed out for my walk. That walk was my way of unplugging and preparing to enjoy the weekend without Hayden.

I wasn't expecting this Friday… this walk… to be any different. Until I opened the door and saw Tage standing on the other side. With a yelp, I slammed the door in his face and leaned against it.

"What's the matter?" Knight asked as he rushed down the hallway.

I pointed to the door as I whispered, "It's Tage."

"Girl," Knight clutched his chest and inhaled deeply, "Don't scare me like that no more, Harlem. I thought something was seriously wrong with you."

"Something *is* wrong with me!" he didn't take my yelling seriously, so I locked the door and grabbed Knight's hand. "Knight, make him *leave.*"

My heart was pounding against my rib cage. Just as hard, as rapid, as loud as a moth's wings – but Tage was an old flame that I wanted to fly away from… not to.

"He must really need to talk to you for him to show up here, Harlem. Hear him out."

"But I… you… what… will you stop walking and listen to me?!"

Knight's back as he walked away turned my frazzled discomfort to anger. In the beginning Knight couldn't stand Tage. Well, he couldn't stand the way Tage was treating me and Hayden. Now he tolerates Tage.

"Hayden isn't here," I said through the door as I leaned against it.

"I know. I came for you."

"Tage…"

"I told you I need to talk to you, Harlem. Just hear me out and I'll leave."

"You couldn't text it to me? Tell me over the phone?"

I felt my face twisting up in sheer distress as Knight returned to the door. *Finally*, I thought to myself. He's about to save me.

"No, Harlem. I need to tell you this face to face. I'm not leaving until you talk to me."

Knight grabbed the back of my shirt and pulled me behind him. He opened the door and I smiled as I buried my head in his back.

"Page," he spoke with a nod and a hint of humor in his voice.

Out of the past two close to three years, I can only recall three times that Knight called Tage by his real name. At first it irritated both me and Tage, but now it's kind of like their thing.

"Knight."

Surprising the hell out of me, Knight pulled me around him, pushed me out of the door gently, and slammed it in my face.

"Talk to that mane," Knight ordered while he locked the door.

"Knight!" I beat on the door with both my hands and feet but that didn't make him open it. "You better open this damn door, or I'm telling Charlie on you when she gets back!"

"So! I ain't scared of her!"

"Knight, open the door!"

"No!"

I called Knight every name I could think of under my breath as I beat my head against the door softly. There was no point in prolonging the inevitable. As much as I didn't want to, I was going to have to face Tage. Right now.

Huffing out a frustrated breath, I turned slowly to face Tage. Okay, well maybe not to face Tage, but to face his feet. I wasn't ready to see his face yet.

"I won't hold you up. You were about to head out?"

"No. Yes. I was going to go for a walk."

"Cool. I'll go with you."

Looking to the side of him, I started walking down the trail. By the time we made it to the side of the house I asked, "What's up, Tage?"

"Still can't look at me?"

"Did you come to talk or be looked at?"

"Both."

Tage wrapped his hand around my wrist and stopped my walking. His hand went from my wrist to the front of my shirt. Using it to pull me closer to him, Tage's free hand went to my cheek. He lifted my head and coaxed me into looking at him.

God I missed looking at him.

So much so that my eyes watered immediately as I looked his face over.

Everything about him was the same... but different. More... potent. More... mature? Older. Defined. Whatever it was it had me even more aware of his presence and that's the last thing I need.

His hair was still just as thick, long, and tightly coiled. He had it pulled up in a huge ball on top of his head. There were a few curls hanging in the back from him scratching and pulling them out I'm sure. His cashew colored skin was just as smooth. Plump lips. Strong clean shaven jaw. All the same. So were his slightly slanted tea brown eyes.

I know this is going to sound corny, but Tage's eyes were the exact brown of my favorite cup of green tea. Just as deep. Just as strong. Just as bold. Just as smoldering. Those eyes used to wake me up and put me sleep just like my tea.

Tage was tall. 6'2. In high school he had a six pack, so I can't even imagine what he has going on under his shirt now! The rest of his body was just as muscular yet slim.

"I miss you, Harlem."

His voice... still had the same effect it had on me years ago. It still made my eyes close. Heart flutter. Body shiver.

"We talk about Hayden all the time."

"No," I removed myself from him and started walking again. He followed, "I mean... I miss *you*."

"Tage..."

"I got an apartment."

I looked over at him briefly as we continued our relaxed stride.

"Why? Just for the summer?"

Tage shrugged. His thumbs slid into the front of his sweatpants and he cupped the rest of his fingers together.

"Maybe. Maybe not. I'm thinking about coming back home."

"Why, Tage? Your father would die, revive himself, then kill you if you left Alabama."

I'm glad he found humor in what I said enough to chuckle, but I was dead serious. Everett was selfish and not all the way there in the head. On top of that he was an angry drunk. There was no way in hell he'd be okay with Tage dropping out of school and not going to the NFL. Tage was his meal ticket.

"I'll deal with that when the time comes. For now, I'm thinking about my future. I gotta make it good because it precedes Hayden's future. That's my main focus right now. I wanna be with my son on a daily basis, Harlem. Not just every weekend. That shit is played out."

My head lowered as I fought my smile. Was I hearing things? This couldn't have been Tage speaking. Taking responsibility and making Hayden a priority. Yea, I'd wanted this from the jump, but not at the expense of Tage not fulfilling his dream. I didn't want him resenting Hayden or me because of that down the line.

I stopped walking and turned to the side to face Tage.

"Tage, that's… great. You don't know how long I've wanted to hear you say this. For you to put forth this effort. But I don't want you to stop doing what you love just to be closer to Hayden. You coming home every weekend to be with him is a lot more than some father's do who live in the same city as their children. What would your plan be? Would you go to The University of Memphis and play there? Your full scholarship is for roll tide. Would you be able to get the same full ride at another school?"

Tage scratched his eyebrow while looking over me at the river. When his eyes lowered and met mine he spoke.

"I don't give a damn about that school or a scholarship, Harlem. I don't give a damn about football. I'm tired of that shit anyway. You know what I've always wanted to do."

That was true. Tage wanted to fly. In all areas of his life. That's why I couldn't understand how he could walk away from his son, but this was the Tage I knew. The one that wanted to succeed and soar. Now he was putting that same effort into his relationship with Hayden, and I couldn't ask for anything more.

Like I could literally die in this moment I was so happy. Well not die, but you know.

"So what are you going to do, Tage? Go to school to become a pilot?" he shrugged and placed his hands in his pockets as he stared at me. Looking over every inch of my face while licking his lips. "Tage…"

"You're beautiful, Harlem. You've always been so beautiful to me. I could never take my eyes off of you."

"Focus, Tage."

"Yes. Yes. Flight school. I got a job at Downtown Aviation. I'm going to see about enrolling there by the time the summer is over. The only thing that has me going back and forth in thought is the money. I'd make a hell of a lot more money playing football, and that would set Hayden up for life… but I'm starting to feel like my presence in his life is more important than money."

Before I could stop myself, my arms were around him and I was hugging him. He wasn't able to hug me back. I pulled myself away from him quickly and ran my hands down my face.

"Sorry. This is… I'm really happy about this, Tage. Of course I want you to do what's best for you because ultimately that will lead to you doing what's best for Hayden. If you think that's returning to Memphis and going to flight school, I will support you one hundred percent."

He licked his lips, then they lifted into a small smile.

"That's what I needed to hear. I'll let you go. Scoop Hayden up."

"Okay. Have fun. Keep him for as long as you'd like. Well, not for too long, but if you want to keep him for an extra day or so that's cool."

His smile turned into a chuckle.

"Thanks, Harlem."

I nodded and watched as he walked away. I wanted him to walk away. Needed him to walk away. Maybe… just… not right now. Not in this instant. I mean… we'd already made it halfway around the trail. Might as well finish it. The hell am I saying? I wanted nothing to do with him when he first got here, now I didn't want him to leave?

Bullshit.

We were *not* going there.

I refuse.

When I heard the purr of his Mustang I waited until it was out of hearing distance before walking back to the house. Charlie was getting out of the car with Knight Jr. I wanted Hayden. I wanted to be able to hold him close. Hug him and feel the love that could only come from him. I needed him to get me out of my feelings. Without him, KJ would have to take my love.

I walked over to Charlie and KJ and picked him up. He hugged me just as hard as I hugged him. Charlie followed behind as I walked into the house. Placing kisses all over KJ's face.

"What's wrong, sweetheart?" Charlie asked with concern dripping from her voice.

"Nothing."

"Then why are you crying, Harlem?"

Her fingers wiped away tears that I didn't even realize had fallen.

"Tage just left."

"Oh. Wow. What was that about?"

I kissed KJ once more before sitting him on the couch. Knight walked in and kissed his wife and son before looking down at me.

"You good?"

Ignoring him, I turned to face Charlie and stared at her until she caught what I was throwing her way.

"Knight, what did you do?"

"I didn't do anything, Charlie, I *swear.*"

Charlie was a sweetheart. She hardly ever had an attitude or let anything make her mad. In fact, the only time I ever really saw her put someone in their place was if they messed with her family. Hayden and me included.

"I don't believe you, Knight. Take KJ upstairs and pull his clothes off so I can get the truth from Harlem. I'll deal with you later."

Knight laughed a guilty laugh as he put KJ on his feet and walked him to the stairs. She waited until they were gone before she asked me what was wrong again. Since my mother was gone, most of my problems were talked through with Charlie. I have an older sister, Carmen, but she stays in Atlanta. She went there for school and never came back home.

I talked to Knight about some stuff, but as a man, he thought logically about everything. Which was cool. Sometimes I needed advice that was black and white. Then, there were times like this when things seemed a bit… gray. That's where Charlie came in. She helped me sort through my emotions, then gave me sound advice.

"Tage is thinking about coming back home. Says he wants to be with Hayden on a daily basis."

Her smile was bright and wide as she grabbed my shoulders and shook me softly.

"That's great, Harlem! So those were happy tears then?"

My head shook as I breathed deeply. Tage wasn't about to get another tear out of me.

"No. They weren't."

Charlie's hands fell. Her head tilted. She looked at me with confusion covering her face and the sight made me smile.

"I'm not understanding, Harlem. I thought you'd be happy. Isn't this what you've wanted? For Tage to be around more?"

"Well, yes, but…" my head lowered as I twirled my fingers around each other. "It's great that he's stepping up. If he really wants to do this, I'm very happy. And I know Hayden will be too. But…" her hand went to my back and that just made me feel even more emotional, "I don't want to love him again, Charlie. And I know that's what's going to happen if he comes back home. I've been doing as good as I have been because he's been so far away. How am I supposed to watch him be active in Hayden's life and it not make me fall even more in love with him?"

Charlie sat back in her seat. Remaining silent as she thought over my dilemma. After a little while she took my hands into hers and said the last thing I wanted to hear.

"I know you probably want me to give you hope that how you feel for him won't reappear, but I can't, Harlem. The thing about love is… it's rude. It's inconsiderate. It has no sense of distance or time. It doesn't discriminate, and it for damn sure doesn't take wrongful pasts into consideration. When love wants to love it will devour you. It will consume you. Fill you and force you to overflow onto whoever it sees fit. If that's now… if that's Tage… there's nothing you can do to avoid it," she kissed my hands and smiled. "All you can do is prepare."

TAGE

The entire drive to my parents' home I kept thinking about Harlem. How it felt to have her arms wrapped around me. Even if it was for less than a second. That half a second was long enough to have me smiling and feeling better than I have in years. She can act like she hates me and doesn't want to have anything else to do with me, but Harlem will be mine.

I came for my son.

But I also came for my woman.

I felt like nothing could ruin my mood when I pulled up to my parents' home, but that thought was quickly put out at the sound of my pops voice. If I could hear him yelling all the way outside, I couldn't imagine how scared Hayden was to be in the house with him. I *told* them about doing this shit in front of my son. All I asked was that he not drink on Friday's before I got home to get Hayden, and his ass couldn't even do that!

As soon as I walked into the house and saw Hayden sitting in the middle of the floor crying his little eyes out my blood started boiling. It took all the Jesus within me to grab him and his bag off the couch and ignore my parents. They were arguing off to the side of the living room like there wasn't a child present. Arguing ain't even the right word. My pops was yelling and my mama was just standing there taking that shit. As always.

Without even speaking to them, I quickly walked back outside. At the sight of me, Hayden stopped crying immediately. He laid his head on my chest and squeezed my neck tightly.

"Sorry about that, young man. I got you now."

I kissed the top of his head and temple as he held me tighter.

"Tage!"

Ignoring my mother, I put DenDen in his car seat and shook my head in disappointment. This was one thing I didn't miss while I was away.

"Tage," her hand tugged at my arm. "I'm sorry, baby. I tried to get him to wait. That's what he was clowning about, but you know how he gets."

Not wanting him to come out and cause a scene, I turned to face my mother and spoke quickly to her.

"Hey. It's cool. I just don't want Hayden around that shi– that stuff. I'll stop by and see you later. Get back in the house before he comes out here tripping."

She nodded and wiped her face. I got in the car and she blew Hayden a kiss. He turned his head away from her and the sadness that covered her face cracked my heart. This was her fault, though. Time and time again Everett Jr., my big brother, and I tried to get her to either leave him or make him go to rehab. At this point I was tired of feeling sorry for her. My patience was running thin. And apparently Hayden's was too.

Two songs into our drive Hayden was back to himself. Singing along to the PnB Rock I had playing. Since I didn't have any furniture in my apartment I took him to the park for a few hours until EJ got off work. Then we grabbed some Chick-fil-a and headed to his place.

After he ate, Hayden crashed. All that running around at the park did him in. Normally I'd try to make him stay up so we can kick shit, but I didn't mind him taking a nap today. It gave me time to talk to EJ about our parents.

"Y'all staying here tonight, or you going back over there?" EJ asked as I came back into the den from putting DenDen in the bed.

"Here. I'm not trying to have him around that mess. As soon as I pulled into the driveway I heard him yelling."

"I know. Mama called me. Said he was yelling about not being able to have a drink in his own house because your kid was there."

That sounds like some shit he'd say. Blaming Hayden for something else that was completely out of his control. Who drinks an entire bottle of liquor before noon anyway? EJ stood and left the room. He returned with his weed and a blunt. After rolling it and lighting it up he offered it to me but I declined.

I had already cut out my drinking after Hayden was conceived, and I didn't smoke when I was around him.

"Has she said anything about rehab, EJ?"

His head shook as he took a pull from the blunt.

"Nah. He still isn't trying to hear anything about it. I told her that if she threatened to leave him he'd go, but she thinks that's going to make him worse. She doesn't want to take a chance on that happening," I unleashed my hair for the first time today by removing the elastic band I had holding it up. "What's up with you, though? You staying here the whole summer? You can crash in the guest room."

"Nah. Preciate the offer but I got my own apartment. My furniture will be delivered tomorrow."

"An apartment? What kind of lease you sign for three months?"

I chuckled quietly as I scratched the side of my ear. Harlem was the only person besides him that knew about my apartment, and even she didn't know for sure how long I was going to be staying around.

"My lease is for a year, Everett."

Catching onto what I was saying, EJ put the blunt down and turned slightly to face me.

"How are you going to stay in Memphis and go to school and play football in Alabama? Pops know about this?"

"No, and you're not going to tell him either. Or mama."

"So what you gon' do, Tage?"

"I got a job at Downtown Aviation," his eyes were rolling and his head was shaking before I could even finish. "I figure I can get in good there, go to school, and work towards what *I* want to do."

"I'm all for that, but is that really what you're going to do? You know how you get with him. When he finds out that you left Alabama for good he's going to flip. All it takes is for him to lay the guilt trip on you and you end up doing whatever the hell he wants you to do. Or he talks about how he's depending on you. I just don't want you to mess yourself up, Tage."

"I've messed myself up enough living for him!" I whispered harshly trying not to wake Hayden up. "That's what messed me up. Doing what he wanted me to do. I'm tired of that shit, bruh. Tired of it. My son is getting big and I'm missing shit hundreds of miles away. It isn't fair for Harlem to have to take care of him by herself because I'm out here trying to live a dream that isn't even mine. It's his."

EJ shook his head, but it wasn't because he didn't agree. It was because he knew the bind I was putting myself in going against our fathers' plans.

"Just... when you tell him... make sure I'm there. How does Harlem feel about all of this? You tell her yet?"

Now that returned my smile.

Harlem.

Looking at pictures of her in no way compared to seeing her in person. Her hair was in its signature braid style. The kind of big chunky braid that wrapped around her head. Made her look like a goddess. Like a Queen. Her gingerbread brown skin was just as smooth and edible looking.

She had the face of a doll. So innocent and angelic. Didn't matter how old she got, she still looked young and just... like an angel. *My angel.*

Harlem's eyes were deep brown, and she was always squinting them because she never wore her glasses. I loved when she did that. Made her look cuter than she already was. Her lips were the same color of her skin almost, and they were so soft and juicy. Those lips... her eyes... her long wavy hair... her slim toned frame... it all got me in trouble.

"She said whatever I think is best for me she's going to support."

"Look at you... blushing and shit."

"I am not blushing."

"Yes you are. You still love that girl, don't you?"

"Was I supposed to stop?"

Our smiles fell, but his returned.

"Not at all. Not at all. All Ima say is this... I let you get away with not being around for Hayden when he was first born because I knew you had to choose to father him on your own. I love that little boy like he's *my* own. *I'm* the one that's there when you aren't. Don't come back home and fuck up all the good Harlem has going for herself and Hayden. If you want to be a father be a father. A consistent father. But don't you play with that girl's heart, Tage."

"I'm not. All I want to do is make me better so I can be better for them. Both of them. In every way they'll have me."

HARLEM

"Why are you giving me such a hard time, Harlem?"

"Because I don't like you, Tage."

I expected that to put out his fire, but it didn't. If anything that seemed to make it burn more.

"But do you love me?"

"That doesn't matter."

"That's *all* that matters."

I wasn't expecting to have this conversation when I came to pick Hayden up from Tage's apartment. He showed me around the place and it was nice. Very clean, open, and spacious. He still had some decorating to do, but knowing him he wouldn't be doing too much. His apartment was a one bedroom, but since it was a loft he was using the upstairs extra room for Hayden. It was cute.

The effort.

The room was too.

I'm guessing Tage thought that since he was back home for the summer, forever, for however long he decided… that things would just go back to being normal between us. Not true. Yes, I was glad that he was trying to be here for his son. But that in no way took away all of the hurt, shame, anger, sadness, and betrayal I felt when he left us. When he left *me*.

As far as I was concerned, him moving back to Memphis was to better his relationship with Hayden. That didn't have shit to do with me.

After he showed me around his apartment he asked if I wanted to kick it with him. I said no as nicely as I could, but he just wouldn't drop the shit. Like he expected us to become this happy family that spent time together and shit. No. Like, picking DenDen up from him instead of Patricia was a big enough step for me. I wasn't ready to spend time with him outside of that.

"Look, Tage, I'm happy you're home… for Hayden… but that's as far as this is going to go. You spend your time with him. I spend my time with him. There is no mingling and in between."

He took a step forward.

I took a step back.

"You telling me you don't plan on ever spending time with me, angel?"

I was rolling my eyes and crossing my arms over my chest before he could get *angel* out completely. He started calling me that when we first met. Stopped after I told him about Hayden. Hadn't heard it since. Until now. It used to make me blush and pine, now the sound of it just irritated my soul.

"Don't go there, Tage. Just move from in front of the door so we can go."

His back was to the door blocking my way out. Hayden was standing in the middle of us. Holding both our hands. Looking from me to him. Smacking on a piece of gum that I told Tage he couldn't have. I don't know why they never listen to me when I tell them not to give him certain things! Hayden chewed on a piece of gum for all of two minutes before he was swallowing it and asking for another piece!

"I'll let you go when you answer my question."

"And what question is that?"

"Do you love me?"

He took another step forward, and instead of stepping back I looked around him to see if it was enough room for me to squeeze through. It wasn't.

"Of course I love you, Tage. You're the father of my child."

"That's not what I mean and you know it."

He took another step towards me.

I took another step back. Grabbing Hayden, I put him at my chest and in between me and Tage so he couldn't get any closer to me. He smiled and nodded as he took a step back.

"You won't be able to use him as your shield all the time, Harlem. Remember that."

That was fine. I'd deal with that when the time came. For now, I rushed past him and out of his apartment. Tage had already taken Hayden's bag out to my car, so all I had to do was put him in his seat and we were on our way out. Instead of going straight home I stopped by my mother's grave.

My mommy died when I was six. She had diabetes and stroked out. In her death, she gave life. Life to Charlie. She requested that her heart be donated to Charlie 10 years before Knight even knew who she was. Charlie had been struggling because of heart failure for most of her life, and the minute my mother saw her she wanted to help Charlie. Ten years after my mommy died and gave Charlie her heart, she met me and Knight. The rest as they say is history.

Knight already wasn't coming home much because he was playing in the NBA, but after she died he really didn't come around. We talked and he sent money home, but that's about it. He didn't settle down in Memphis until I got pregnant.

Carmen stayed with me and my daddy until she was 18, then she left for college. Hasn't been back to stay since. She's so caught up in her own life that she hardly even knows what's going on in mine. And Hayden barely knows her. He knows that that's his TeTe Carmen but that's about all. He speaks to her when I call her, or when we go visit her, then he goes into his own little world avoiding her.

Hayden and I made ourselves comfortable at my mother's grave, and I thought about my life as I always did when I came to visit her. Couldn't help but wonder how differently my life would've been if she was still here. If I wouldn't have had to grow up so fast. Learn how to take care of myself so soon. Feel so grown and alone. Feel such a need to be loved. Would I have fallen for Tage as quickly and deeply as I did?

None of that matters now.

Things may have started out rocky when I first found out about Hayden, but we're sailing pretty smooth now. And I refuse to let Tage and his inconsistent ass come in and mess that up.

I wasn't supposed to go to the store tonight, but one of my girls called in sick. I always liked to have at least two associates in the store at all times, so I had to suck it up and go in. Knight and Charlie were having date night. My daddy had KJ, and he seemed to lose a little of his mind when he had both boys at the same time. I took Hayden to the store with me and called Tage to see if he could watch him until I was done at the store.

Normally in situations like this I'd call EJ, but when I called he reminded me that Tage was in town. Ha. Isn't that funny? I'd completely forgotten that Tage was here. I was so used to not having him around for stuff like this that he didn't even cross my mind. As slow as things were in the store I could've just kept Hayden up here, but I was sure that after six things would pick up and I didn't want him in the back unattended.

About 20 minutes after I called Tage he was walking into the store drawing all kinds of attention to himself. His hair was down and he was looking so damn good without even trying to. I used to love running my fingers through his curly hair. Oiling his scalp.

No.

No reminiscing.

"Well damn. I wish my man looked like that and came here to buy *me* stuff," Mahalia, my associate said before biting down on her lip.

"Stop that. That's my baby daddy."

She pushed my shoulder so hard I almost fell over when I bent down to get Hayden's attention, but she grabbed my arm and kept me from doing so.

"I'm so sorry, Har! I just can't believe… did you say… *that's* your baby daddy?"

Ignoring her, I spoke to Hayden as I closed the coloring book he was scribbling in.

"Your daddy's here, DenDen. You're gonna go with him for a few hours until mommy gets off work, okay?"

Hayden nodded before kissing me and standing. I walked him in front of the counter and gave his hand to Tage.

"Thanks for coming on such short notice. I'll come get him as soon as I lock the place up."

"No rush. He can stay the night with me if you want. Keep you from having to come out my way."

Although I appreciated the gesture, I wanted my baby with me tonight. He'd already been with Tage for the weekend, and with the way Tage had me in my feelings… I needed to hold Hayden tonight instead of the teddy bear I usually slept with.

"Mm mm mm," I heard come from behind me.

I turned in time enough to see Mahalia looking Tage over as she licked her lips.

"Get fired if you want to, Mahalia. Get fucked up."

"I'm sorry. I'm just… gonna… go check the fitting rooms."

"Yea. Do that."

"Cut that out," Tage said with a smile as he tugged at my arm to regain my attention.

"You need to go. Got all these females drooling over you."

He smiled, which he hardly ever did, and that lightened my mood. It wasn't that he was an unhappy person. He just had a natural mug on his face most of the time.

"You know I don't care about any of that shit."

That was true. Because of how Tage looked and how talented he was I expected him to be cocky. A flirt. A cheater. But none of that was the case. He was the sweetest thing in life. I always felt like my heart was safe with him. Maybe that was the problem. Maybe I trusted him *too* much.

"Yea, I know. I'll um, call you in a few hours. Maybe around 10."

"Cool."

He didn't walk away. He just stood there staring at me.

"Tage…"

"I'm sorry. Just making up for lost time," Tage looked over my head, then shook his before kissing my forehead softly. "See you later, angel."

"Angel? Ugh. Lucky ass," Mahalia muttered behind me.

That's why he kissed me. Because she was looking. He was always doing little things to prove to me that I was the only one he wanted.

"Don't be kissing my mommy, Daddy. That's *my* mommy!"

"I can kiss her. She was mine before she was yours."

"She's mine now!"

"We can't share?"

Hayden shrugged as he looked back at me, and I couldn't help but smile and get all proud and teary eyed.

"No. I want her allllll to myself."

Tage laughed, and so did a few customers that were standing around.

"Stingy ass lil boy."

"Don't be cursing at my baby, Tage."

Tage nodded and threw his hand up in surrender.

His lips still felt the same. Still just as soft. Yet firm. And moist. I waited until my boys were out the door, then turned to face a visibly jealous Mahalia. This was going to be a long night.

#

It was hard, very hard, but I was finally able to talk Harlem into grabbing a bite to eat with me. Technically it was Knight and Charlie that convinced her after five minutes of going on and on about her never doing anything without Hayden and needing to start living a little. Instead of making her come and pick DenDen up, I let her go home and I dropped him off. By the time we made it to their house he was knocked out. I took him to the room he shared with Knight Jr. and put him down, then took a chance on asking Harlem to ride with me.

I didn't realize I hadn't had anything to eat today until I walked into their home and my stomach started talking to me. I don't know what Charlie cooked earlier, but the shit had the whole house smelling good as hell. We walked to my car in silence. She was pouting with her arms crossed. Squinting and trying to walk ahead of me knowing damn well she couldn't see in the dark without her glasses on. As soon as she reached for her door I locked it.

Her head flung back and she cursed under her breath while shaking her head. Knowing how mean she could be, I tried not to laugh when I walked over to her and placed my hand on the door handle. Harlem avoided my eyes until she realized I wasn't going to open the door and let her in until she looked at me. When she did, I opened the door for her and she got in.

For the most part the ride to Waffle House was silent. Every time I tried to talk to her, her petty ass would cut the music up louder. Yes, I expected her to give me a hard time but damn. She was not making this easy for me. The car hadn't even come to a complete stop before she was hopping out and heading to the restaurant. I started to take my time getting out and meeting up with her to give myself time to mentally prepare, but when I saw her heading towards a pot hole I got out and jogged over to her.

Harlem stepped right into the hole. I might not have been quick enough to keep her from twisting her ankle a little, but I was able to grab her and keep her from falling. Her hands gripped my arm securely as I held her and put my mouth to her ear.

"If your blind ass would stop being so difficult I'll lead you and guide you. Don't break your neck out here being stubborn. I'm not dealing with Knight and Hayden because you walking fast in the dark knowing you can't see without your glasses."

Tightening my grip around her, I lifted her into the air and pulled her out of the hole. Harlem looked to the right and left of me before mumbling, "Thank you," under her breath and starting to walk away. She must've thought about what I said because her head hung as she stopped walking and looked back at me.

I held my hand out for her, and instead of her putting her hand in mine she wrapped it around my pinky and held on to it.

Good enough.

Harlem chose a booth in the back of the restaurant and I happily slid in next to her. Her mouth opened in protest, but she closed it and looked out of the window.

"So what's up, Harlem? What's been going on with you?"

Slowly, she turned and looked into my eyes. Hers lowered to the smile I was wearing, and finally... *finally*... she gave me a small smile. The way mine widened you'd think she just gave me winning lottery numbers. That's how it felt, though. Like I'd just hit a jackpot I didn't even know I was playing for.

"You're not gonna give this up are you?"

"Not at all. I just wanna make you smile, Harlem. I know I can't take back all my fuck ups, but I at least want to try and fix them," my pointing finger slid down her nose softly and she lowered her head and smiled again. "Let me."

"Fine."

Our waitress came and took our drink orders. This is where we used to come after all of my games, so we knew what we wanted without even having to look at the menu. She ordered orange juice, an order of sausage, and hash browns with cheese, jalapeño peppers, and ranch dressing. I got water and the all-star special with extra cinnamon raisin toast because she always used to end up eating mine. The waitress, Holly, repeated our orders then left, and I wasted no time returning to our conversation.

"So…"

"What do you want me to say, Tage?"

"Tell me about everything I've missed. How was prom? Graduation? What school are you going to? What's your major? How's Princess? Are you seeing anyone?"

Harlem smiled and licked her lips as she shook her head slowly.

"Prom was cool. Me and Princess went together actually. Graduation was cool. Felt good to be done with that chapter and onto the next. Knight's big overgrown ass acted a fool when my name was called. Crying and yelling my name and shit.

I'm going to The University of Memphis. Majoring in Marketing. I want to go into marketing research, public relations, or advertising. Not sure yet. More than likely public relations, though.

Princess is well. Still wild and crazy. She's going to TSU in August. No I'm not seeing anyone."

"You're single?"

"Out of everything I just said *that's* what you want to focus on?"

I waited until Holly placed our drinks on the table and left before I answered.

"Yes. Why are you single?"

"I don't have time to date. Even if I did… I just don't want to."

"Why not?" she didn't answer me. Just looked at me like I should already know the answer to my own question. "So there's been no one since me?"

"How was it in Alabama? How was your first year of college? Any advice?"

"Harlem…"

"*Please*, Tage."

"Why can't we talk about this?"

"Because I don't want to!"

Her lips trembled, but she licked them and bit down on the bottom one to cover it up. She took in a deep breath and swallowed hard.

"I'm sorry, angel. I didn't mean for things to end up like this."

I covered her left cheek with my hand and caressed it with my thumb. When she didn't push me away I pulled her into me and kissed her right cheek.

"I'm sorry, Harlem," I kissed it again. "For everything."

My nose brushed against hers as I repositioned myself to face her.

Harlem closed her hand around my wrist and looked from my eyes to my lips. She licked hers and if I didn't know any better... I'd say she leaned in closer to mine. Her eyes went over my head, and the sound of Holly's voice ruined my flow. Harlem scooted away from me as Holly apologized for interrupting. She set our food in front of us, asked if we needed anything else, then left.

"Harlem..."

"Can we just not, Tage? Please. You hurt me. You left me. You made me feel like I didn't mean anything to you. Like I didn't matter. Like the child we created didn't matter. That's that. There's nothing that you can say or do to change the fact that you hurt me. To my *core*. It's *over* for us. Just focus on Hayden. That's how you can fix things and at least keep things friendly between us. Just do right by DenDen."

"I understand your pain and your position, but ain't nothing friendly about us, Harlem. When I saw you that day in the hallway I didn't think *I wanna be her friend*, so you can kill that *right* now. I get it; I have a lot of making up to do and work to put in, but you out your damn mind if you think it's over for us."

Harlem pushed her food to the center of the table and crossed her arms on top of it.

"You not gon' eat?" I asked as I put half a piece of toast in my mouth.

"Shut the hell up, Tage."

HARLEM

Today was the longest day ever. Hayden was super cranky this morning. He gave me a harder time than normal getting ready. That crankiness carried over while he was at daycare, and I ended up having to go up there because he hit one of the other kids over a toy. When I went to see what the hell was wrong with his mean, crazy ass he burst into tears talking about he wanted his daddy.

His daddy.

Tage had orientation for his new job over the weekend, so he couldn't spend as much time with Hayden as he normally did. I didn't want to pacify Hayden and award his bad behavior, but I couldn't deny my baby of his father if that's what he truly wanted.

This was new to all of us.

If it was hard for me to get used to having Tage around more consistently I can't imagine how Hayden was dealing with the change. But, I'd rather Hayden have an attitude because he wanted Tage than for him to be acting out because he didn't.

So I called Tage to see if he could pick Hayden up from daycare and spend a little time with him. He agreed and ended up texting me after he picked DenDen up. I couldn't really text him back because we were crazy busy at the store, and Ashley called in yet again. On top of being shorthanded, having to deal with crazy customers practically fighting over discounted prices, and worrying about Hayden, I had two high school girls try to steal from me!

They straight up tried to steal from my store!

To put it mildly, by the time I got home... I was drained. Mentally, emotionally, and physically. I was hungry as hell, but before I could even eat I had to smoke and clear my mind. Knight and I started smoking together when he caught me going through his weed stash right after I had Hayden. There was no point in him trying to keep from me smoking. I'd been doing it since I was 14, and if our father couldn't stop me he couldn't either.

His solution was for me to smoke with him to be sure that what I smoked wasn't laced with anything.

As I made my way out to the patio I told him that I was about to light up if he wanted to join me. When Knight came outside he was holding a bag from Edible Arrangements, and my mouth immediately started to water.

"You got these for me," I asked reaching for the bag.

"No."

Knight took the blunt from my hand while I used the other to open the card hanging from the bag to read it.

Hope this makes your day a little better, angel. – Tage

The weed was no longer necessary at the sight of that card.

"Dammit, Tage."

After putting the bag on the ground, I opened the box that was inside and found my favorite. White chocolate covered strawberries. The first time I had these Tage and I were out and about shopping. We passed Edible Arrangements and I wanted to go inside. He bought me a box of strawberries that were dipped in white, milk, and dark chocolate.

White chocolate was my favorite.

About a week later, I had a box sitting at the front door when I got home from school.

After that he'd randomly have a box delivered when I'd least expect it.

I hadn't had any since things changed between us.

They became one of those bittersweet things you try to avoid.

"Knight, can you go? I have to make a phone call."

Knight blew smoke out of his nose and mouth before answering me.

"How you gon' make me leave my back porch? You told me to come out here anyway."

"You can come right back," I whined while shoving him out of his chair.

I waited until he was back in the house before I pulled my phone out and dialed Tage's number. Tage answered, and the phone was filled with laughter. His and Hayden's laughter.

"Aight hold on, baby boy. Mama's on the phone," Tage said into the receiver.

"Hey, Mommy!"

Why was I getting teary eyed? I hardly ever cried, but Tage and Hayden... especially together... could put me in my feelings easily.

"Hey mommy's baby! Hey, Tage."

"What's up, Harlem?"

Scooting down in my seat, I began to take the halo braid I'd been rocking down.

"You bringing my baby home tonight?"

"Hadn't planned on it. You want me to?"

"You can keep him. I was just... going to thank you in person for the strawberries. That was very sweet and thoughtful of you, Tage. Thank you."

"No problem. Seemed like you needed a little pick me up."

"I did. Thank you."

"Harlem?"

"Yea?"

"Come over."

"Tage..."

"No funny business. You said you wanted to thank me in person anyway, right? Come over."

"Well that was only if you were coming over here. Not me going over there."

"The hell is the difference, Harlem?"

"It's other people here."

"You don't trust me? You don't trust yourself to be alone with me?"

"No."

"What do you think I'm going to do? I'm not going to try to have sex with you or no shit like that. I just want to spend time with you and my son. Together."

And that's what I was scared of. Sex wasn't my concern. Falling for him again was. Growing closer to him was. Feeling like a real family was. Giving Hayden an artificial copy of the true love and bond that I wanted between me and Tage was.

It was best this way.

Him having Hayden.

Me having Hayden.

Us having him together yet separate. Apart from each other.

"It's better this way, Tage."

"Better for who?"

"…For… Hayden."

"Bullshit. Us being together is what's best for Hayden."

"Fine, so maybe it's better for me."

Tage exhaled loudly into the phone and I could imagine him scratching his eyebrow in frustration.

"That's cool, angel. Whatever you need. Ima let you go, though."

"You mad at me?"

"Yes, but I'm mad at me too because this is my fault. It was foolish of me to think I'd be able to come home and we'd be this perfect, happy family. Happy couple. You're worth the fight, Harlem. I have no problem fighting for you. For us."

I damn near jumped out of my seat when I asked, well yelled, "Where was this fight when I needed it, Tage? When I needed you to fight for me? For our family? Where was the fight then? I'm good now. I don't need it and I *don't* need you."

"But I need you. I…"

"No. Don't. Don't you *dare* say you love me. You *don't*."

"Fuck it. Say goodnight to Hayden, Harlem."

A second or two passed before Hayden's sweet voice was filling my ear, and I couldn't even speak right away.

"Mommy?" Hayden called.

"Yes, baby. I'm here. Goodnight, sleep tight, don't let the bed bugs bite."

"Night, Mommy. I love you."

"I love you, DenDen."

"Now tell daddy goodnight and don't let the bed bugs bite and sleep tight and goodnight."

"Hayden, wait…"

Tage was silent, but I knew he was on the phone because I heard him breathing.

"Tage?"

"What?"

Now he had an attitude. That was cool. After all he'd put me through... he deserved a few sleepless nights and attitudes.

"Don't be mad at me. Goodnight."

He hung up in my face! Petty ass. I couldn't help but laugh as I shot him a text.

Don't hang up in my face no more with your petty ass.

Baby daddy: I'm done with you for the night. You hurt my feelings.

Join the club.

Baby daddy: I'm coming to get my strawberries back.

They'll be gone by the time you get here!

Baby daddy: That wouldn't surprise me. Goodnight angel.

Goodnight Tage.

TAGE

Between the money I'd saved over the years from my stipends while I was in high school, my refund checks from my first year in college, and the money I made betting on games I really didn't have to work over the summer. Getting a job at Downtown Aviation was more about my future than my present. Being able to put them on my resume when I was done with school would definitely better my chances of landing a job with a major airline.

After my second day of work, I stopped by my mama's job to have lunch with her. Just like me, she didn't have to work, but she chose to. It was her way of getting away from my pops for a little while. He wasn't always a nasty, hateful drunk. Let my mama tell it, he was a nice and charming man until he allowed his addictive spirit to ruin his life and career.

Everett Sr. was the first in our family to make it big. He was drafted by the 49ers and became the first internationally known athlete of the Young family. Between the women, drugs, and alcohol he ended up getting benched more than he was played. Thanks to a few commercials and sponsorships, he was able to stack some bank before he was benched for good.

His reputation preceded him, and although he was traded to a few teams over the years, his attitude just fucked him up. The last team he was on the roster for was the New York Giants. They kept him on their reserve list for two seasons before releasing him.

Money and fame changed him. My mother was the only person that stayed by his side, and she was paying for her loyalty every day of her life.

Because he ruined his football career he wanted to live through mine. He tried through Everett Jr. first. When that didn't work he focused on me. He gave me everything I asked for. Everything I wanted. Everything I needed. Even things I didn't want or have a use for. Football became my life. It's what I ate, breathed, lived.

There wasn't time for anything else when I was in middle and high school.

I wasn't allowed to go to the movies, parties, or hang out with my friends.

If I wasn't practicing I had to watch games and meet with coaches, players, and scouts.

I had more money as a teenager than most adults because his way of pacifying my desire for a normal life was to throw money at me. Money that I really didn't have the time to even spend and enjoy. Now it was like he expected me to pay him back all that he'd given me. That money came in handy when Harlem got pregnant, though.

Harlem.

She was my escape.

She was the only thing worth risking it all for in my eyes.

She was the reason I'd skip practices and lie about where I was going.

She was the reason I'd skip school to spend the day with her.

She was the reason I'd tell him we were practicing after games just so I could spend a few hours with her.

She was the reason I'd tell him I was going to training camps or having meetings at my coach's house and end up at hers.

She was my relief.

The only person that made me feel like I didn't owe them something.

Like they wanted me for me; not what I had to offer them.

Like I was more than a future check they could cash in on.

Harlem was the one that treated me best.

Harlem was the one I treated the worst.

I had to make things better between us. She deserved better. Harlem was putting up one hell of a fight, but I was committed to winning her back. The key to her heart – Hayden and Knight. If I wanted to get to her, I'd have to go through them. At the sight of my mother, I pulled my phone out to text EJ. He would meet up with Knight and Charlie's brother Rodney for drinks sometimes. Knight hated me less than he did when we first met, but he still wasn't my biggest fan. If I could get him to help me get Harlem back, there's no way she could deny me. After sending EJ a text asking him to put something together for later tonight, I stood and hugged my mama.

"You brought my favorite?" she asked as she sat down.

I picked up two steak burritos from Las Delicias on the way.

"Yes ma'am. How's your day going?"

She shrugged as she opened her to go box.

"Pretty good. Working a double shift tonight, so I'm thankful for this food. How about you?"

"You can have my burrito for later then, and it's going good. I actually wanted to talk to you about some shi– some stuff."

Her eyes shifted to mine briefly, but she quickly returned them to her food while she cut into her burrito.

"What's going on, Tage? Does this have anything to do with the fact that you aren't staying at home or with EJ?"

"How you know I'm not staying with EJ?"

"Because when I went over there the guest room was spotless and the bed was made. He tried to cover for you, but I can tell when you're staying somewhere and when you're not."

I chuckled and sat back in my seat.

"You got me. I'm not staying there."

"Then where are you staying?"

"Westgrove apartments."

Her chewing stopped then started back slowly.

"With who?"

"Myself."

"What are you doing, Tage? Why would you move into an apartment just for the summer? You could've saved that money and came back home."

"I've been saving my money for years. Besides, I couldn't come back home after experiencing living on my own," I scratched the side of my eye and studied hers before I continued. "And... I need my own place anyway. I don't plan on going back to Alabama."

She placed her fork and knife in the to go box. After pushing it to the side she leaned into the table.

"What do you mean you're not going back to Alabama?"

"I mean I'm not going back to Alabama."

"So you're going to school here?"

"Yea."

"I don't know, Tage. Your father really wanted you to go there because of their football team. He's not going to be pleased with you playing for The University of Memphis."

"I'm not playing for them either."

"Then who are you playing for?"

"It doesn't seem weird to you that your only concern about my education is the school's football team, Ma?"

"Of course that's not my only concern. I just know that you'll get a good education anywhere. It's a bit harder to find a great football program. Especially one that's offering a full ride."

My elbows went on top of the table. I massaged my temples and tried not to get aggravated.

"Well good because I'm going to Downtown Aviation."

"Downtown Aviation?" she shouted. "Downtown Aviation, Tage? Are you out of your mind? Everett is going to kill you! Do you know how much he's invested in your football career? How hard he's worked to get you to where you are? He's depending on you, Tage. You can't throw all that the both of you have worked for away for some silly hobby. That's what flying planes is. Your hobby. Football... that's your life. That's what you need to focus on making your career. And with things getting harder around the house... his money is running out, Tage."

"Then he needs to stop sitting around all day drinking and get a fucking job."

"Watch your mouth."

I stood and placed my hands on the table.

"I expect him to not understand. You on the other hand... I expected more from you, Ma. I expected you to be happy for me. Be happy that I finally have the courage to live my life for me. Why is that so hard for either of you to do? Is money *that* important to you? That you'd rather have that than my happiness?"

"Of course not, Tage. Sit down. Please. Hear me out."

"There's nothing that you can say to change my mind."

"I'm not going to. I just want you to understand where I'm coming from."

I didn't want to, but out of respect for her I sat back down and heard her out.

"Your father wants you to take advantage of your talent and opportunity because he didn't. He was basically blacklisted in the NFL and that made him bitter. When I had EJ he was *so* proud. Proud because he had a son that could carry on the tradition of Young excellency that he dropped the ball on. Yea, Everett was the first person in the family to reach that level of success, but you know what mattered to him most?"

"What, Ma?"

"Pleasing his father. Instead of his father seeing him as a success for making it to the NFL, he saw him as a failure for not being able to stay. So Everett wanted to redeem himself through his boys. He wanted you all to live the life he couldn't. He wanted you all to have the success he couldn't. He wanted to be proud of you in the way that he wanted his father to be proud of him.

Your grandpa Seal was a mean, ungrateful, and finicky old man. He'd tease your father about his drinking and inability to play, but expected Everett to have all of his bills paid come first of the month. It didn't matter how hard Everett tried, Seal always found something to complain about. It was when he couldn't get his father's approval that he started seeking it from other people.

Other men. Other players. Other women. The entourages… they fed his ego. They made him feel good about himself. So he spent all night and day partying with them because they made him feel good about himself. And that seeking of approval is what led to his downfall. Everett just wants what's best for you…"

"But football isn't what's best for me, Ma. It may be what's best for him, but it's not what's best for me. That's not my life. Not my dream. I don't want that. I'm going after what I want. I want to fly. I want to be here for my son. For my girl. That's it. I don't need the millions. I don't need the fame. I don't need any of that. That's not the only way to be successful to me. You know what success is to me? Fulfilling my passion and my purpose with those I love by my side. All I need is my family and to fly. If that's a letdown to him then it will just be a letdown to him, but I can't live my life for him anymore. I'm sorry. He shouldn't even want me to after what grandpa put him through."

"I hear you. I do. And believe it or not I want you to do what's best for you. If that's flying… you have my blessing. Just do me a favor and don't say anything to your father about it right now. Like I said he's running out of money and expecting you to be his payout. I'm afraid he'll take a turn for the worse if he finds out you're taking up flying."

"Is that why you're working double shifts tonight? I can help you with money, Ma, but I'm not going to fund his habit."

"No, I'm fine. I have money saved. I'm working to avoid having to deal with your father."

"Why won't you make him go to rehab?"

"I'm working on it. He says he's going to go to rehab so he can try and find a job as a sports commentator or coach, but he just won't let up. There's really nothing that I can do, though, Tage. He has to come to that conclusion on his own."

"Maybe we need to have some kind of intervention."

"I'm willing to try anything at this point."

My phone vibrated in my pocket, and I was pleased with the text from EJ. He reached out to Knight and they were going to meet at Sticks for a few games of pool.

"Well, I'll talk to EJ about it and see what we can come up with. I gotta go, Ma."

"Okay, baby. I love you."

Standing, I took in my mother's restless face, baggy eyes, and loaded smile. Shit had to change. Soon. My father was toxic, and if she wasn't going to stand up to him… I would.

"I know, Ma. I love you too."

"I'm surprised you came, dude. What's up?" EJ spoke.

He stood and we shook hands. I did the same with Knight and Rodney before taking the last available seat at their table. We made small talk and played a few games of pool, then I saw my opening with Knight.

The subject of betting came up and EJ was trying to explain why he'd always go for the team I betted on. In this instance, I was betting on the home team. It was the second quarter and the Grizzlies were losing by 30 against OKC, but that didn't stop me from betting on the Grizzlies. I sat back in my seat with a smirk as EJ talked passionately about my skills.

"I'm just saying; Tage is a beast. I don't know how he does it but he always wins. Doesn't matter what sport he always wins. The last bet I played on the strength of his suggestion paid for my car. Cash. So if he says the Grizzlies are going to win I don't give a damn if they're down a hundred, I'm betting on Grizz."

"There's no way in hell they're going to come up 30 and beat OKC. Period," Knight replied.

"You wanna bet?" I asked.

As a retired Grizz himself and their current announcer I was surprised Knight didn't think they would win. Like most people he allowed how far behind they were to cause him to doubt them. I guess because of the current position I was in with Harlem, I was more empathetic with anybody or any team that was fighting for a win.

Knight was still loyal to his team, though. Had he not made his family a priority and cut back on announcing every game he'd be with them now.

Knight sat back in his seat and stared at me silently. He finished off the last of his beer before nodding slowly.

"What you wanna bet?"

"If the Grizzlies win you have to help me get Harlem."

Both EJ and Rodney's faces screwed up on the sides of me, but I didn't turn to face either of them. My eyes remained locked on Knight's.

"And if they lose?"

"Your choice."

"If they lose… you leave her alone. Stay around for Hayden, but you leave Harlem the hell alone."

"Tage…"

I lifted my hand to silence EJ. Looking at the game, Conley had just missed another three, and the Grizzles were now down by 36.

"Bet."

Knight smiled… as if he knew something I didn't. The entire table was silent as we watched the game. The second quarter ended and the Grizzles were down by 24. During halftime Knight asked me to play a game of pool. Now I will say this, I might be good at choosing winners, but Knight could play his ass off when it came down to pool. He was one man I wouldn't bet against.

Knight racked 'em and broke 'em, sending the yellow and blue solids in immediately.

"I was 16 when Harlem was born. She was the most beautiful baby I'd ever seen," he said before sinking the red solid. "When our mom died I wasn't there for her like I should've been," he sank the burgundy solid. "I came home and she was 16 and pregnant. I promised her then that I would always be here for her and never leave her again."

He sank the purple solid.

"The second I found out about you I wanted to beat your ass for getting my baby pregnant. Then you took what seemed like forever to man up and take responsibility for the child you helped create and that made me want to kill you," orange solid sunk. "You know what stopped me from doing either?"

I shook my head as he put his last solid, his green solid, in the pocket closest to me.

"Because she begged me not to," Knight put his pool stick on the table and stepped towards me. "It was the day after she was able to bring Hayden home. Harlem hadn't heard from you since she gave birth. I was literally sitting there on the edge of her bed while she rocked Hayden and cried over you.

The entire time she did I was putting bullet after bullet after bullet in my gun. I was going to kill you that day, Tage. But I spared you because Harlem loved you. She *loves* you. As much as she hates what you did to her... she loves you. And I love her. There's nothing she can say or do to spare you twice. If you don't plan on sticking around and doing right by her leave before she opens up to you. So this is the first, last, and only time you will get this warning – hurt my baby sister again and I will kill you. Are we on the same page?"

"I'm not trying to do anything to Harlem but love her. That's *it*. Hell if I mess it up this time I'll hand you the bullets myself."

Knight ran his hand down the back of his neck and nodded as he thought over my words.

"Ima hold you to that."

"Fine with me."

We played another game before returning to the table. Drinks were flowing all around me. They were laughing and having a good time while my eyes were glued to the TV. I couldn't breathe easily until the game was over. Until I saw the final score that showed the Grizzlies won. Two quarters later they won by five points. The Grizzlies won – and so did I.

HARLEM

"I'll be on my best behavior. I promise."

Tage was leaning against his doorframe giving me the biggest puppy dog eyes he could muster. Hayden was standing in front of him trying to do the same. The plan was for me to come and pick Hayden up after the spa trip that Tage so graciously paid for, head home, then fix something to eat. When Tage didn't protest to me picking Hayden up early I should've known he was up to something. Now he was trying to get me stay while he fixed dinner.

Any other time I may have said no, but I was so relaxed after my massage and mani and pedi that I couldn't even put up a fight.

"Fine," I gave in while stepping back inside of his apartment.

"Really?"

Tage locked the door behind me with disbelief apparent in his voice and on his face.

"Really."

"It worked, DenDen. Can you believe it?"

Hayden nodded with a wide smile as he followed Tage into the kitchen.

"What are you cooking?"

In his living room, I sat in the middle of the couch and made myself comfortable. My shoes came off at the same time as my purse.

"Blackened catfish, sweet potato fries, and broccoli."

He wasn't slick. I loved blackened catfish. Sweet potatoes were Hayden's favorite. How did he know that, though? Had he been talking to Knight or Charlie? No way was this a coincidence.

When I cut the TV on it was already on Nickelodeon. As soon as SpongeBob's voice filled the living room Hayden was running out of the kitchen and making his way on the couch with me.

"That's how we're doing it, Hayden? You just gon' leave me in here to cook by myself for SpongeBob?"

"Yes, sir."

"So disloyal."

I gave Hayden a quick kiss on the cheek before standing and going into the kitchen. The sight of Tage cooking was one I thought I'd never see. It was kind of sexy. I wouldn't tell him that, though.

"What are you up to, Tage?"

He turned slightly to look at me, but returned his attention to the fish he was seasoning.

"Why I gotta be up to something?"

"Because I know you are."

Tage shrugged and walked over to the stove.

"Maybe I just want to eat with you and Hayden. No big deal."

"Blackened catfish, though? You just happened to decide to cook my favorite today?"

"Maybe."

He placed his hand a few inches over the skillet to gauge its heat before adding two pieces of fish to the skillet. The loud crackling had me thinking he had the heat up too high, but I figured he knew what he was doing so I didn't say anything about it.

"Either way, this is a very nice gesture."

Tage put the plate that once held his fish down and turned to face me.

"You think so? I get points for this?"

I smiled and took a natural step in his direction.

"Yes, you get points for this."

The crackling was even louder, and I started to smell the fish a lot sooner than I should have.

"Eh, Tage. You might wanna turn the heat down under your fish before you burn it."

"I ain't gon' burn it. You gotta have the heat high so the outside will be nice and crispy."

"Tage... maybe for fried fish, but I really think you should turn the heat down."

Tage turned back to the stove and cursed under his breath at the sight of his fish.

"Thin ass fish. How is it burning and sticking to the pan already?"

"Did you put oil in the skillet, Tage?"

He cut his eyes at me and it took all the self-control I had to keep from laughing. I walked behind him and watched as he scraped the fish from the skillet. What started out as him trying to flip it to the other side turned into the fish sticking and breaking into multiple pieces. Not able to hold it in anymore, I laughed as I grabbed the skillet and told him to get me a metal spatula.

By the time I was done getting all of the fish off the skillet Tage muttered, "Well, he said blackened was your favorite," while staring at the burnt pieces of fish.

"Tage... blackened... as in with seasoning. Not black as in burnt to a crisp."

"Mane, forget you, Harlem."

He snatched the plate from my hand and walked it over to the trash can, making me laugh even harder as he pouted.

"I'm just teasing you, Tage."

Trying to hold my laugh in, I walked over to where he was standing and grabbed his hand.

"I wanted it to be special for you."

"This is special. I really appreciate the effort, Tage. I think you trying to cook was very sexy. And you being all sad over burning it is cute."

"You think I'm sexy?"

"You trying to cook was sexy."

Tage licked his lips and smiled.

"I'll take that. Guess I'll order a couple of pizzas. Find out what kind DenDen wants while I clean this shit up."

I returned to the living room with Hayden and he wanted pepperoni as usual. Tage ordered one pepperoni pizza and a Hawaiian BBQ pizza. An order of cheese sticks completed our order. About 20 minutes later we were chowing down while watching *SpongeBob*.

I never thought I could find pleasure in something as simple as eating pizza and watching cartoons, but this... this was honestly the most fun I'd had in a while. Every so often I'd feel Tage's eyes on me. When I looked over at him he'd look away. This went on for six episodes before Hayden was hopping off the couch and stripping out of his clothes.

"Is he... I know he is not getting butt naked in the middle of this room. Harlem... what is going on with your son?"

"Oh, now he's my son?" I grabbed Hayden and put his socks and shirt back on. "He just does this when he's sleepy. He's ready for his bath and story then bed. Ain't that right, baby?"

Hayden nodded before resting his head on my chest.

"Y'all don't have to leave. It's dark out. Just stay here for the night."

"It's fine. I have my glasses in the car. We'll be fine."

"Are you sure, Harlem? You can take my bed. I'll sleep on the couch."

"I'm positive. It's fine."

It was obvious he didn't want to agree, but Tage nodded and stood.

"Fine. I'll carry him out. And you better hold my hand walking down these steps too."

With no protest, I took ahold of his hand when we got outside and let him lead me down the stairs to my car. As he put Hayden in his seat I got my glasses out of the glove compartment and put them on. I walked over to my side of the car and Tage opened the door for me.

"I don't know why you never have these on. They put you on another level of fine, angel. Give you that sexy librarian vibe."

Tage's finger slid across the top of my glasses before I pushed it away with a smile.

"Today was fun, Tage. Thank you."

"You're thanking me for burning fish?"

"I'm thanking you..." my smile fell as I considered whether I wanted to complete my statement or not. "For reminding me that you aren't all bad."

He closed the door and leaned against it.

"I'm not."

"I know. I guess I just need reminders."

"I have no problem giving them to you until you can trust me again. And even then I'll continue to prove that you can trust me, Harlem. All I need is a chance. Fuck that. All I need is time; I'll take my own chances."

Here I was... getting all teary eyed again. Fighting to keep them in again. Fighting not to fall for him again.

"You left so many stains," I said more to myself than him as I clutched my heart.

"Let me clean them, angel. Let me fix it. Please."

His hands were on my cheeks. Pulling me into his chest. Lifting my head to face him.

"Mommy."

His nose was brushing against mine.

"Let me fix it, Harlem."

"Mooommmy."

"I need to get him home and in bed, Tage."

"Promise me you won't shut down on me when you leave here."

"Maaaaaaa!"

"*Okay*, Hayden."

"Promise me, Harlem. I need you to stay open for me."

"I have to go."

I pulled myself away from him and kept my head lowered until he opened my door again and stepped away from it. Tage opened the backseat door and kissed Hayden.

"You owe me for messing up my flow, young man."

Hayden nodded and pushed Tage's face away from him while trying to rub sleep from his eye. After closing the door, Tage made his way to me again.

"Can I have a goodnight kiss from you too?"

"I don't think that's very appropriate, Tage."

"I don't give a damn. I wanna kiss you."

No matter how much I hated to admit it, I was still attracted to Tage. Not only did thoughts of kissing him cross my mind frequently, but thoughts of making love to him did too. Didn't matter how much I hated him… there was one part of him I'm sure I'd always love. His dick.

"Ta—"

His lips came so close to mine I just knew he was about to kiss them, but he didn't. He kissed the side of my mouth, then pulled himself out of my car.

"Goodnight, angel. Let me know when y'all make it home."

"O… okay."

Tage closed the door and I forced myself to start my car and reverse. I didn't want him to kiss me. I mean I was expecting it, but I didn't want it. So why was I mad because he didn't?

TAGE

I have no problem fighting for Harlem. It's only fair. But damn. She wasn't even trying to meet me on the battlefield. Two weeks had passed since I tried and failed to cook her dinner, and I just knew that things were going to loosen up between us.

Wrong.

She still had the same guards up.

She still wasn't trying to give me no kind of play.

I will say this, though, she was spending more time with me when I had Hayden. Just like today. We had a little family day. We took him to Chuck E. Cheese and to the mall. While at the mall we made an appointment to take some pictures. All three of us. When I dropped them off at the house I asked her to ride with me to my cousin's birthday party and she said no.

No.

Because going out at night would be too much like a date.

Knight told me to give her the space she needs to battle it out within herself about how she feels for me. He told me to let her take the lead and to fall back until she was ready for me to pursue her. That was the best advice I'd gotten in a while because I swear I don't know how much more of her rejection I can take before I give up.

Not because I don't want her anymore, but because I *do*.

And it hurts like *hell* for the one you want to not want you.

If I made her feel half as bad as I do right now... maybe I don't deserve a second chance.

Fuck being a family man. Tonight, I'm going out with my boys and enjoying myself. And if Harlem wants to rot away in the house... so fucking be it.

"Yo… you will not believe who just walked into the spot," Jordan yelled into my ear over the music.

Jordan was my best friend. We'd been at my cousin's party for all of 30 minutes before I gave in and hit his blunt. Now I had my own blunt in one hand and a bottle of 1800 in the other. This female whose name I don't even remember asking for was grinding all against my dick and here he comes face checking messing up my shit.

"Does it look like I care right about now, Jordan?"

With my blunt between my lips, I ran my hand over ole girls' ass before smacking it. She grabbed my thigh and looked back at me with a smile.

"My dude, it's lil bit."

The blunt fell from my lips immediately, hitting ole girls' ass before hitting the ground. Lil bit. That's what Jordan called Harlem.

"Ow!" she yelled while grabbing her butt cheek.

"Stop tripping. You didn't feel that. You wouldn't have even known what it was if you weren't looking back."

I pushed her to the side slightly and grabbed the blunt, trying to search the room for Harlem casually in the process. The hell was she even doing here? She said she didn't want to come, so what was she doing here?

My eyes landed on Princess first, and to the right of her stood Harlem. I would say she looked beautiful, but that seemed like too common of a word to describe her. The white shorts and crop top that she wore made her melanin ooze. Baby looked like a gingerbread brown goddess. Harlem was slim, but she was curvy, and the pumps she had on had her calves and thighs looking right.

Even with anger lacing her face she looked angelic. She looked like she couldn't hurt a fly, but I knew better than to believe that. Harlem was a beauty with a beast in her.

I handed my blunt and bottle to Jordan then headed over to Harlem. Rationalizing the situation didn't make me feel relaxed as I walked over to her. Technically she had no reason to be mad because she kept insisting that there was nothing nor would there be anything between us. So she shouldn't have a problem with me dancing with or even talking to another woman. Somehow me going over that in my head didn't calm my nerves at all.

"Har–"

Her hand covered my face as much as it could and she mushed the shit outta me! I grabbed her wrist and used it to turn her around and pull her back into my chest.

"What the fuck is wrong with you, Harlem?" I asked as I walked her out of the house.

"You can let me go."

"Nah. Not until you answer my question. Did you just mush me?"

She ignored me. Her hands tried to pry my arm from around her waist unsuccessfully.

"Harlem…"

"Let me go, Tage."

"Why you putting your hands on me?"

"Why you putting your hands on *her*?"

Slowly, I unraveled my arm from around her and turned her to face me.

I missed her.

I missed this Harlem.

The one that cared.

About me.

The one that wanted me.

"Tage?"

Her skin was so beautiful. So brown. So smooth. So perfect.

"You said you didn't want to come. What are you doing here, Harlem?"

She crossed her arms over her chest as her bottom lip poked out a little. I missed those lips too. Missed the way they felt. How they tasted.

"I wanted to surprise you. I called Princess and told her to come through. Looks like I'm the one that was surprised, though."

Those eyes. Those deep, rich brown eyes. The kind of eyes that snatched ya and held you captive.

"I of course don't want you to see me with another woman like that... but damn, Harlem. I just need some affection."

And that hair. That long wavy hair. I missed pulling it. Running my fingers through it.

"That's fine, Tage. Just because I'm single and not trying to date doesn't mean you have to live the same way. You're free to do whatever with whoever."

"Then why did you mush me with this little ass hand?"

I couldn't resist. I had to grab it. I had to pull her closer. I had to kiss the back of her hand. Kiss her palm. Kiss her fingers. One. By. One. Her eyes closed. Her mouth opened partially. Her breathing increased. By the time I made it to her ring finger she pulled her hand away from me and opened her eyes.

"I got... temporarily... in my feelings. Seeing you with her. Made me..." she crossed her arms over her chest again. "I was mad. Possessive. Maybe even a little jealous. But I was out of line for that and I'm sorry. I'm gonna grab Princess and leave. You enjoy yourself, Tage."

Harlem tried to walk past me, but I grabbed her arm and pulled her back into me.

"Can you just let yourself feel something for me for once, Harlem? Besides anger over me leaving? At this point I'd rather you be mad about seeing me with another woman than that. As fucked up as that sounds... at least it shows me that you still feel *something* for me. You do... don't you? Can you let me know that I affect you at least half as much as you affect me? *Please.*"

Her head lowered as she shook it. She pulled her hand out of my grip and took a step away from me.

"For almost three years, Tage, I had to put up with you being unsure of what you wanted. How you felt. What you were going to do. And you mean to tell me you can't even handle a month of me not giving in to you?"

"I'm not saying it's fair, but I don't know how much more of this I can take."

She chuckled and took another step towards the door.

"Trust me, Tage, you don't have to take it at all."

HARLEM

When your two-year-old sends you to your room for having an attitude it's time to reflect on life. Seriously. Hayden straight up called me out on my attitude and told me that I was being mean and that hardly ever happens. Not towards him. Not without a reason. Even when I punish him I end up crying and being more emotional than him. But today I was being a lot more snippy than usual. With him and everyone else in the house.

And at my store.

And it was all Tage's fault.

Seeing him dancing with that girl over the weekend really messed with my mental. It was one thing for me to deny him and know that he was home alone like me, but seeing him with someone else put things on a whole other level. I should've expected that to happen eventually. Why wouldn't it? He's gorgeous. Sexy as hell. Sweet. Downright charming when he wants to be. Playful and romantic, but he's got that streak of bad boy in him. Ugh. Tage was perfect. *Was.*

Until I saw firsthand his flaws. His desire to please his family so much that he disappointed others. His tendency to run away from his problems instead of solving them. His tendency to withdraw and disconnect from things and people until he was ready to engage.

And you know what? That should've been fine. Because we all have flaws. We all make mistakes. We all have those things about us that we aren't so proud of. He was human. But you know what fucks with me? The fact that I can't seem to accept those flaws and love him unconditionally.

Yes, I want Hayden to grow up with both parents in the home. Yes, I want to do all that I can for him to have the family unit that I didn't have after my mother died.

And to be even more honest, I miss Tage. I want Tage. But I hate Tage. No matter how I try to read my bible and pray that I be able to get past this and forgive him I can't. I see him and I think about what he did and I just... get so angry. Then I get sad. Because who am I that I can't forgive him when Jesus forgives me? Am I better than Jesus? Am I so holier than thou that I can cast my stone sinlessly?

"Sweetheart?" I looked up to find Knight and Hayden standing at my door. "Hayden wants to give you something."

Knight ushered Hayden into my room, and Hayden looked back at Knight with unsurety as he walked to my bed. Hayden's short arm extended, and in the middle of his little hand was a cookie. There was no need for me to ask where it was from. I could tell just by looking at it. It was a chocolate chip bar cookie from Ricki's cookies. My favorite. Knight would always get them for me after he pissed me off or when I was in a mood.

"Thank you. Both."

"There's more in the kitchen whenever you're ready to come out."

"Thanks, Knight," he nodded and was about to walk away but I stopped him. I waited until Hayden had left the room before I asked, "Can I talk to you?"

"Always."

Knight closed the door and walked over to my bed. We both sat on the edge of it and I tried to think of a way to express my question as straightforward as I possibly could. That was the only way Knight's brain worked. He didn't do the guessing, open ended, roundabout conversations.

"Why do I feel like Tage expects me to just... get over my hurt in an instant to spare his feelings?"

He chuckled then smiled at me sweetly.

"Because he does. Let me say this first... I don't want you to ignore what you feel. I don't want you to think you aren't entitled to how you feel. That you don't deserve to make him work for this and fight for you because you do. I want you to make him work to have you, but you're going about it the wrong way.

Men... we don't put much effort into things we believe we're going to fail at. Yes, we like a challenge, but more than that... we like to win. We like to conquer. If a man believes he can win you he will chase you, but if he doesn't think he's going to win you or be successful at loving you he won't pursue you.

I've talked to Tage and he's honestly at a point where he thinks he has no chance of getting you back. He's losing hope. And if he loses hope it doesn't matter how much he wants you he's not going to risk being rejected by you and hurt again."

"I just don't understand why, though. He rejected me. He hurt me!"

"But you're a woman, sweetheart. You are an emotional being. You handle your emotions far better than he *ever* will. That's not to say that as a woman you should be hurt because you can handle it better, but that's just how it is. That's our nature. As a woman, you are stronger emotionally than a man. Just as Tage is stronger than you physically you are stronger than him emotionally.

You adapt to how you feel. You become aware of how you feel and handle it quicker than a man. It takes more out of Tage for him to process and handle his emotions than you. You can't expect Tage to handle things the way you do. What you can handle he can't and what he can handle you can't. You're more focused on feelings and experiencing and handling those feelings in this moment while Tage is focused on the end results. The end goal. Let me give you an example – the walk you take every Friday... why do you do that?"

"It relaxes me. Helps me unwind. Kind of like a habit. Something I do for myself."

"Okay, and what about when I go for my run in the morning? Why do I do that?"

I smiled and bit down on my lip as my eyes watered.

"To stay in shape."

"Exactly. You walk for the experience. The ritual. The feeling of relaxing and unwinding that you get from walking. I run to stay in shape. To reach a goal, a desired effect. You're emotion..."

"You're logic. I get it. We're not on the same page. I'm focused on feelings and the past and he's trying to figure out what the hell we're going to be in the future."

"Right again. Tage has only one thing on his mind – getting his family back. That's his focus. That's his goal. It's not that he doesn't understand or respect your feelings, it's just that he can't see things emotionally and logically at the same time."

"So what should I do?"

"I want you to be completely honest with me… do you want him back?"

Be honest with him? Hell, I needed to be honest with myself.

"All hurt aside, Harlem. Pain aside. Past aside. Do you want him back?"

I exhaled deeply. For 13 Mississippi's all that could be heard in my room was the ticking of my clock. For years I'd battled my feelings. Battled my desire for him. I was ashamed to want him because he hurt me. Left me. Didn't seem to want me. I thought I'd never admit to loving him. Liking him. Wanting him. Ever again.

But the truth of the matter was…

I did want him.

I did like him.

I did love him.

He was my first love.

My first heartbreak.

My first lover.

"I do. I do want him back. But I'm just so scared and I feel so stupid for wanting him."

"Love makes you stupid sometimes, but I honestly don't believe this is one of those times. I don't think he meant to hurt you intentionally. I think he was just… a boy with a man's weight on his shoulders and he didn't know how to handle that. But he's trying to fix it now, sweetheart, and that's what matters most. That he's learned from his mistakes and grown from them. You know I wouldn't be sitting here talking to you about his ass if I didn't see any growth in him, but I do."

"So what should I *do*?"

"Talk to him. Be honest with him about how you feel and what you need from him in order to move forward. Make him work for his place in your life… but ease his mind and let him know that he *has* a place in your life. That's all he needs. That confirmation. That peace of mind. If he knows that you haven't completely given up on him… he will never give up on you. You give him that place in your life and let him prove that he deserves it. If he doesn't… I'll take care of that."

"No, boo. If he doesn't that will just be the end of us, but I don't want you getting involved."

Knight gave me one of those *yea right* chuckles as he stood.

"I'm serious, Knight."

"I am too. If he messes up this time, well I probably shouldn't tell you. Just in case I get caught and they make you testify."

"Knight!"

Knight ruffled the top of my hair with the palm of his hand and stared down at me for a few seconds before walking away. When he got to my door he said, "I love you, Harlem, and I'm proud of you."

"I know, boo. I love you too."

He nodded and left. Knight was right. Tage and I were on two completely different pages. It wasn't fair of me to try and get him to understand what he'd put me through. Quite honestly, he never would be able to. I either needed to let him win me back and move forward or let him know that he had absolutely no chance and let it go completely. But this half in and out dwelling on the past trying to get him to feel what I feel just isn't going to work.

He would work for me no doubt, but in return... it was only fair that I made him aware of what the prize would be. Me.

Feeling a little like me again, I grabbed my phone from the middle of my bed to call Tage. As the phone rang I stood and headed out of my room and down the hall.

"What's up, Harlem?"

"Can you come over?"

Tage and I had our best talks in the car when we were in high school, and as I walked out to his car I figured that would be the case tonight too. When we got off the phone earlier he told me he'd be at me in 30 minutes. He made it in 15. By the time I made it off the porch, Tage was out of the car and walking over to the passenger side.

He looked down at me with those tea brown eyes but remained silent. Tage opened the door for me and was about to go back to his side, but I grabbed his hand and stopped him. He stood in front of me... looked down at me... and all of the feelings that I wanted to release started to ripple within me.

It was like he felt my energy because his eyes closed and he groaned quietly. His body weakened. His shoulders caved. His left hand went into my hair and he pulled me into his chest while the right hand grabbed my ass and squeezed.

Tage held me.

Tight.

Close.

Pulled my hair gently and mumbled how sorry he was inside of it over and over and over again.

His hands lowered and lifted. Both resting in the center of my back. Arms wrapping around me like I was his anchor. Like he wanted me to keep him grounded. Keep him steady. Like he wanted to drown. Drown in all that I was feeling. All that I needed to pour inside of him.

And as heavy as I felt when he pulled me into him is as light as I felt when he lifted his head and looked into my eyes.

Every time that he's tried to kiss me before this I denied him, but this time... this time when he brushed his nose against mine I lifted my head just enough to show him that this time would be different. That this time I wanted him to go all the way. To take what he wanted. To give me what I needed.

"Are you sure?" he whispered into my lips, cupping the back of my head into his hands.

On the tips of my toes, my answer was a peck to his lips. A peck that he obviously wasn't expecting because he didn't kiss me back. I opened my eyes and looked into his.

"I'm sure."

Tage returned his lips to mine and kissed me so tenderly... so passionately... I literally felt dizzy. He lowered himself and lifted me at the same time, trying to rectify the height difference, but I didn't care. I didn't care how much I had to arch and lift my neck to get to his lips. Being here... with him like this... was such a needed comfort that I found myself sighing into his lips as I tossed my arms around his neck.

Pulling his lips from mine, Tage gazed into my eyes.

"Not that I'm complaining, but what has gotten into you, angel?"

He pushed my hair out my face and stared into my eyes with such concern it made me laugh.

"I just... can we just... get in the car and talk?"

"Yea. Yea. Sure."

Tage stepped to the side and I got in. After closing the door behind me he got in on the other side. His eyes were on me as he lowered the volume on his radio.

"I want to apologize, Tage, for giving you such a hard time."

"Harlem, no..."

"Hear me out," I grabbed his hand and inhaled deeply. "I know that it was easy for me to choose to keep Hayden because at that point it seemed like he was all I had. My mommy was gone. My relationship with my daddy was all screwed up. Carmen was in Atlanta and Knight was traveling all over and... I honestly felt alone.

Yea, I had you and Princess, but... I didn't really feel like I had any family. Hayden was my chance to change that. But you... you had a lot more to lose. I was so focused on how having Hayden affected my life that I didn't take into consideration how it was going to affect yours. I'm not saying you leaving us was okay, but I understand your reasoning behind it now. And no matter how much that hurt me then, what matters is that you're here now. So, I'm going to try to not hold the past against you anymore, but if you leave again..."

"I won't, Harlem. I give you my word. I'm not leaving him or you. If I leave Memphis y'all will be coming with me. As a family."

I pulled my hand from his and sat back in my seat.

"I don't want you to feel like you have to be with me for the sake of Hayden, Tage. We're a package deal, but we're not. We don't have to be in a relationship just because we have a child together. I want to be with someone that wants to be with me for me."

"You think I don't? Harlem... I love you. I'm in love with you. I know that leaving you made you question that, but I'm here now, and I'm ready and willing to show you with my actions just how much I love you. I couldn't be the man you needed me to be then, but I can now. I am now. I just... needed some time to get my shit together, babe. It has nothing to do with you being the mother of my child.

I regret pushing you away during the process, but I needed to be better for you. I love you for you. I love you because you loved me. Because you saw me when no one else did. Because you accepted me. Supported me. You made me feel like I was more than an opportunity. Like I had more to offer than running the ball. You gave me the freedom to be myself, Harlem, and I honestly have no desire to share me with anyone else *but* you."

"You love me? Still?"

"I never stopped. I always will."

"Tage..." I was scared. Lord knows I was. Lord knows the fear of Tage deciding to up and leave plagued me every day since he returned, but that didn't stop me from confessing, "I love you too. I've missed you so much."

He kissed my lips once. Twice. The third time his tongue slipped inside. Reminding me of how much I loved the taste of him. The feel of him.

"I missed you too. Look in the backseat."

I looked in the backseat and a wide smile immediately took over my face. Wasting no time, I crawled into the back of the car while he got out, walked to the back, and got in like a normal person. Tage rested his back against the door with his long right leg stretched across the seat as best as it could. I found my place in his chest immediately.

Just like old times we talked, listened to music, ate airheads and hot Cheetos, and drank cherry flavored Clear Fruit bottled water until I fell asleep. On his chest. In his arms.

TAGE

Waking up in the backseat of my car with Harlem sleeping on top of me was priceless. Although being scrunched up made the position uncomfortable physically, that was the most peaceful sleep I'd ever had. I started to wake her up right away, but the sight of her sleeping so peacefully combined with the rising of the sun had me stationary. All I could do was lie there and look at her. Run my fingers through her hair, kiss the top of her head, and look at her.

The sun must be her alarm clock because as soon as it was up fully she started stirring. Harlem lifted her head and it shook slowly. Carefully. Causing her nose to brush against my chest. Her fingers gripped my arm and squeezed while she opened her eyes weakly. They squinted and focused in on me, and she smiled immediately.

"Good morning," I mumbled, then cleared the sleep out of my throat.

"Good morning."

Her eyes closed again as she put her head back on my chest. Her arms around my stomach. Like her ass was going right back to sleep. I would have loved to hold her for hours, but she needed to get Hayden ready for daycare and head to work and so did I.

"Angel, you gotta wake up."

"Ion want to."

Her arms held me tighter while she struggled to wrap her legs around me.

"Harlem, we gotta get to work, babe," I said… but that truth didn't stop me from wrapping my arms even tighter around her and locking her in with my legs. I kissed the top of her head again and smiled when she groaned.

"What time do you get off?"

"Five."

"Call me."

"You know it."

Harlem avoided my eyes as she pulled herself out of my embrace. I opened the door and got out, then helped her do the same. We both stretched for a while before walking up to her front door.

"We'll talk later," I assured her. "You know Ima FaceTime you and Hayden when I get to work and I'll text you throughout the day."

Her bottom lip poked out a little and she lowered her head.

"Harlem…"

She wrapped her arms around me and pushed her face into my chest.

"You 'bout to make me quit my job just to stay with you, girl. Gone in that house."

Her grip around me loosened, but it didn't matter because I was wrapping my arms around her to keep her close. She pulled her face out of my chest, then put her chin on it and looked up at me. I kissed her forehead. Her nose. Her lips. Her cheek. Then buried my face in her neck as I hugged her deeply.

"Tage?"

"What's up?"

"If you decide you don't want to do this anymore…"

"That's not going to happen, Harlem. Don't even go there."

With a nod, she inhaled deeply and pulled herself away from me.

"Okay. Have a good day."

"You too."

I stood there until she was inside, then I headed back to my car. Today was going to definitely be a good day.

Halfway into my shift I got a frantic call from my mother. She was hiding in her closet behind her clothes while my pops searched for her. By the time I'd made it to her he was gone. Which made her even more fearful because he was driving drunk. We sat there for three hours waiting. Waiting for *that* call. That he'd been in an accident or arrested. Neither came.

Not able to play the waiting game anymore, I left to search for him. Found him up the block with his car half in a ditch. It wasn't low enough to cause any real damage. It was just enough to keep him from driving any time soon. I started to leave him there struggling to pull the car out of the ditch, but the shit was embarrassing. Him... wobbling from side to side and falling all while trying to literally pull a car out of a ditch with his bare hands.

As far as I was concerned that was the final straw.

It was one thing for him to drink and stay in the house. If my mama wanted to put up with him that can her prerogative. But when he started drunk driving and putting innocent lives on the line things had to change.

I had to pick him up and carry him to my car. The entire ride back to the house I couldn't help but look over at him in pure disgust as he talked to himself and gagged. Floating in and out of consciousness.

When we got back to the house I carried him inside and put him in the bed. Instead of giving my mother his keys I kept them. Whoever she was going to get to tow and fix his car would have to get them through me. Even after the car was fixed he wouldn't be able to drive for a while. Not until he cut back on his daily drinking and committed to going to rehab. That would be a fight when he sobered up in the morning I was sure, but it was one that I was willing to take if it meant keeping his careless ass from behind the wheel.

Before I could even go back to work I needed to get my mind right. I called Harlem and she told me that I could come up to the store to see her if I needed to, but I needed my son. There's something about the innocent, unconditional love of a child that just... makes everything better. They have this way of knowing when you need love and a hug more than you do.

Time after time, Hayden has picked up on my moods even before I do. When I get to thinking about the fucked up choices I've made and how I walked out on him... before guilt can fully consume me... he says or does something that puts a smile on my face.

I don't know everything there is to know about love, but I know that there are a few loves that can't be compared to anything else. The love of God. The love of your soulmate. The love of your mother – when she's a good one. And the love of your child.

The second I walked into the room and Hayden saw me he dropped the book he was *reading* and sprinted towards me. I lowered myself to lift him up in my arms.

"Hey, baby boy."

"Hey, Daddy!"

Hayden squeezed my neck so tight it caught my breath off. I chuckled as I loosened his grip on me.

"You having a good day, DenDen? What were you reading?"

"I can't read, Daddy. I was just looking at the pictures."

"What you mean you can't read?"

He shrugged and patted my hair as I carried him out to my car.

"I don't know. Mommy ain't taught me yet."

"I'll teach you."

"Where we going?"

"Nowhere. I just wanted to see you for a little while."

His head tilted as he looked into my eyes.

"You okay, Daddy?"

My smile was loaded.

"I'm okay, young man."

"You need a cookie? Auntie Charlie gives me cookies and ice cream when I'm sad."

"She does does she? Gone have your teeth rotten before you even get them all."

"I got all my teeth, Daddy!"

"No you don't! You ain't got but four!"

"Nu unh!" he bucked so hard he almost came out of my arms. "I got allll my teeth!"

"But why do you always have to extend your words like that, though, Hayden? You tryna prove a point ain't ya?"

He crossed his arms over his chest and tried to force his smile in like Harlem does when she's mad, and I swear, at that moment... none of what I'd gone through earlier with my fucked up parents mattered. All I wanted to do was be the best father I could to my son. All I wanted to do was cherish this moment that I had with him. And pray that I never became anything like my father.

HARLEM

Tage said he was fine, but I could hear in his voice that he wasn't. It was no secret that he bore the weight of his parents' choices on his shoulders over the years. Between trying to protect his mother and get her to leave and please his father and get him in rehab, he was dealing with far more than any young person ever should. I didn't realize things had gotten as bad as they did because Tage and I weren't talking about anything but Hayden this past year, and when I'd drop him off with Patricia she never let on about what was really going on.

I knew that Everett had a drinking problem, but I didn't know about the abuse. He was quick to try and hit Tage and EJ, but Patricia? Drunk or not... that was unacceptable. When Tage called me earlier he didn't go into detail. Just said that his mother was hiding from Everett in the closet. After he called me I prayed for them and tried to get things done in the store as quickly as I could so I could go and see him.

I left the store, went home and fed and bathed Hayden before putting him to sleep, then headed to Tage. It took him a while to open the door and when he did I saw why. Well I smelled why when he spoke to me.

"I thought you weren't drinking anymore?"

"I wasn't."

"Then why are you drinking now?"

Tage took my hand into his and pulled me into his apartment. He closed and locked the door behind me, then walked into the living room. I followed behind and rolled my eyes at the sight of the half empty bottle of Tequila.

"Tage..."

"I just..." he sat down. Elbows on his thighs. Face in his palms. "Needed to numb myself, angel. I was cool while I was with DenDen but by the time I made it back home and was alone and started thinking..."

I sat next to him and caressed his back with my left hand while pulling his hands from his face with the right.

"You know you could've called me, Tage. This isn't the way to handle what you're feeling. Don't start running to liquor when you can't handle your thoughts and feelings. That's what your daddy did. That's what he does. Is that..."

"You *know* that's not what I'm trying to do. How I'm trying to be."

"So go pour it out."

He looked at me like he wanted to protest, but got up and did as I said. My eyes scanned the walls that were covered with pictures of him in various football uniforms and plaques, yet this wasn't even half of all of his plaques, pictures, and trophies. Most of them were at his parents' home. How could someone who devoted so much of themselves to something just give it up completely? Either his resentment of it and his father ran deep or this was just a temporary break – whether he wanted to admit it or not.

Tage made his way back to the living room. He stretched across the couch and placed his head in my lap. Naturally I started to caress his hair. His face. His chest. He exhaled loudly as I kissed his forehead and covered his heart with my hand.

"I feel like I should be there with her, Harlem. She needs me. She needs help with him."

"You and your father are gas and a match, Tage. EJ needs to be the one over there. He's not as bad with him as he is you. What happened?"

He went on to tell me that Everett had a job interview this morning that he was half drunk for. The man that gave the interview could smell the liquor coming out of his pores and told him immediately that he couldn't take the risk of hiring Everett. Everett went home and drank even more, then started to take his frustrations out on Patricia verbally. When she tried to leave things turned physical. She ran to the closet to give him time to calm down. That's when she called Tage.

Everett left after that and Tage found him at the end of their street trying to get his car out of a ditch. When he left Everett he was asleep in bed and Patricia was at his side watching him sleep as usual.

"Why won't she just leave him?" I asked.

Tage shrugged and ran his hands down his face.

"Same thing we keep asking. She's hindering him and doesn't even realize it. She's so worried about him getting worse that she can't see accepting his behavior will never help him get better."

"Does he know you're not going back to Alabama?"

"Nope, and I really don't know when I'm going to tell him. Never seems like the right time. He's half sober in the morning so I guess I'll have to stop by one day before work, but I just don't know, Harlem. I think it would be best if I waited until he went to rehab and had a clear mind completely. If he takes it hard I don't want her to have to pay for it, you know?"

"I understand."

I continued to caress him. His breathing relaxed. Eyes lowered. My hand went to his ear and I brushed it lightly like I did Hayden's to put him to sleep.

"You always know what to do to soothe me."

His voice was calm and relaxed enough for me to be comfortable leaving him alone tonight.

"That's what I'm here for."

Tage opened his eyes and fully. He pulled me down to him and covered my lips with his. The taste of the Tequila on his tongue had my chest heating up. Like I'd downed a shot. Or was it his kiss? Was it his fingers pulling my hair gently? Or was it the low hums that escaped him every time I pulled his lips into my mouth.

He pushed me away softly and bit down on his lip.

"You need to go, Harlem."

I didn't want to… I needed to. Things were good between us, but we weren't committed to each other again. And even if we were I said I was waiting until marriage before I had sex again. So me leaving was our safest bet.

"Will you be okay?"

"I'll be fine. Thank you for stopping by. I didn't realize how much I needed you until I had you."

For some reason that made me smile. The thought of him needing me. Tage stood and so did I. He walked me to my car and we shared a quick kiss before I left – praying he didn't have another bottle of liquor that he was going to open the entire way home.

TAGE

"I heard Hayden held you hostage yesterday."

I looked over at Charlie and smiled. That was true. Yesterday we went to get his hair cut for our family pictures today. On the way back to the house we stopped and got Harlem a box of strawberries from Edible Arrangements and some roses. Charlie was out working and Knight is on the road with the Grizzlies, so I stayed over for a few hours and kicked it with them.

When I tried to leave Hayden acted a clear fool. I tried to take him with me but that made him cry harder. Harlem tried to take him upstairs with her so I could sneak out and he cried even harder. Over and over again we asked him what was wrong and he didn't answer. He didn't stop crying until me and Harlem sat down on the couch with him in between us. Hayden wiped his eyes and looked at both of us, then he sat in the middle of the floor and started coloring.

He wanted us both.

Together.

And the fucked up part about it was he wasn't even paying us any attention. The entire time I was there he was coloring.

I guess he just wanted us together. Wanted us close.

"Yea. He showed his natural ass, Charlie. Never seen anything like that before."

"He just wanted the both of you at the same time that's all."

"Yea, I don't know, Charlie. I want him to have us both and I want us to be a family, but you think that could turn into a problem? Is it possible to give a child too much of your time?"

"Well, you can spoil a child so much that he becomes attached to you and doesn't want to be around anyone else, but Hayden is past that age. That usually happens when the baby is first born. When the mother or father hold him too much. I think with Hayden he just... isn't used to having the both of you together and now that he does he prefers it that way. I don't think it's anything to worry about, though. When he gets used to the idea of you all being a triune it won't be as difficult for him to let go then."

"I hope you're..."

"*Damn*, Tage."

Me and Charlie looked towards the sound of Harlem's voice. She was standing on the bottom step with her shoes in her hand looking as good as she wanted to look. The white spaghetti strapped dress she had on had blue and pink flowers that complemented the matching pink slacks and jean button down shirts DenDen and I wore. Her hair was in these big, loose curls that flowed down past her shoulders. The shoes she held were gold like her bracelet, necklace, and earrings.

Even her makeup was gold. Made her face look like it was glowing. Like she was glowing.

"You look..."

My eyes went from her face to her waist. The dress clung to her hips and accentuated her perky breasts.

"Beautiful," Charlie supplied, but that never seemed good enough to describe her in my eyes.

She was more than beautiful. She was...

"Breathtaking," I muttered as my eyes returned to hers. "You look breathtaking, angel. Absolutely gorgeous."

Harlem blushed. She placed her shoes on the floor and stepped into them.

"Thanks guys. You look quite handsome yourself. I love your hair like that."

I ran my hand down my head absently. EJ's girlfriend insisted that I have my hair straightened. I agreed only because Harlem liked that shit too, but I made her put it in a low ponytail and braid it up.

"Thanks."

"Let me take a picture before you guys go take your pictures."

Charlie rushed past us and me and Harlem chuckled. I walked over to her, grabbed her hand, and pulled her close enough for me to kiss.

"You look so sexy," I complimented into her lips before kissing them again.

"Don't kiss my mommy, Daddy!"

Hayden jumped off the couch and made his way between us. With all of his strength he pushed us apart.

"Are we about to have this conversation again, Hayden?"

"Mommy, don't let him kiss you. You're mine!"

Harlem smiled as she kneeled in front of Hayden.

"You're right; I am yours, but I'm daddy's too. Just like he's mine and he's yours too. We're each other's. We're a family. It's okay to share me. I will still have just as much love and as many kisses for you."

"Are you sure?"

Harlem kissed his cheeks and smiled harder.

"I'm positive, baby. I will *never* run out of love for you."

Hayden hugged her neck while looking up at me.

"Okay. You can kiss her, Daddy."

I helped Harlem stand as I shook my head.

"Thanks for your permission, young man."

"You guys ready?" Charlie asked as she came down the stairs.

After I picked Hayden up and positioned him in the middle of me and Harlem, Charlie lifted her phone to take the picture, but she lowered it slowly.

"Wow. I didn't realize how much he looks like the two of you until just now. His skin is like the perfect mix of you both. Right in the middle. Harlem, he has your eyes and nose, but Tage's mouth. Their heads are even shaped the same. Same dimple in his chin as Tage. Wow."

I looked from Harlem to Hayden as Charlie snapped away. He definitely looked like her when he was born, but he was starting to look more and more like me. To see someone with half of her and half of me... to know that there was a being that was half of me on this earth. That there was a piece of me outside of me that I could see... that shit was mind blowing.

"Thank you," I almost whispered, feeling myself get a little choked up.

Harlem looked at me skeptically with a smile.

"Thank me? For what?"

"For him. For us. For you."

HARLEM

The pictures came out beautiful! After Tage ordered a million copies of every possible size, we left the studio and grabbed a bite to eat. Now we were on our way to Hayden's favorite place – the park. As Tage drove his hand was in my hair and massaging my shoulder like he always used to do. Just that simple act of him wanting to be attached to me would always make me feel soft. And wanted.

I'd been thinking over what I said to Hayden earlier and it was kind of messing with me. The whole me being Tage's thing. It wasn't that I didn't want us to be in a committed relationship; I was just scared. Not committing and putting a title on this felt easy and less complicated. Made me feel like if he left it wouldn't hurt as bad. It wouldn't hurt as bad because he wouldn't be mine this time so it shouldn't faze me.

But I dan fucked around and said I was his and now I'm starting to overthink it while he probably hasn't thought twice about it. Or committing to me. He just seemed to be riding the wave. I wish I could be that relaxed and carefree about the situation.

"Ayyye that's my song," I yelled as I cut the volume up.

Ella Mai's "Boo'd Up" had become my theme song. I played it so much Hayden knew exactly when to come in with the heartbeat bridge. I turned slightly in my seat and started singing to Tage.

"Feelings so deep in my feelings. Know this ain't really like me. Can't control my anxiety," he started cheesing and shaking his head, *"Feeling like I'm touching the ceiling. When I'm with you I can't breathe. Boy you do something to me,"* my fingers slid down his cheek as his eyes lowered. He looked over at me briefly and bit down on his lip. *"Ooh no I'll never get over you until I find something new that get me high like you do. Ooh no I'll never get over you until I find something new that get me high like you do. Listen to my heart go..."*

Hayden wasted no time jumping in.

"Badu boot up... beedee dadu boot up."

"Listen to my heart go..."

"Badu boot up... beedee dadu boot up."

Me and Tage cracked up!

"Y'all crazy as hell, mane."

"Whatever. You just mad because you don't know the words to sing along."

"Damn right. I feel left out."

"Fine. I'll find something you know the words to."

"PnB Rock!" was Hayden's vote.

"Cool. I know like three songs by hard. Let me see."

I went through his songs on my phone before settling on "Notice Me." That one song turned into a full karaoke session starring all three of us. I laughed and smiled so hard for so long my cheeks were hurting by the time we made it to the park.

Tage came to open my door. I expected him to move and open the door to get Hayden out, but his body remained close to mine as he looked down at me.

"I appreciate you giving me a second chance at this, angel. I know we're not committed and I'm not going to rush you... but you got me. I promise you that."

Why did that make me feel bad? So bad I couldn't even speak. Like he was more invested in this than me.

TAGE

My 20th birthday was right around the corner, and instead of wanting to wild out with my friends all I wanted to do was spend the day with my two favorite people. Harlem and Hayden. My 20th birthday was right around the corner, and instead of me feeling light and carefree I felt weighted down by my parents' issues.

I had to leave work yet again because my mother called. This call was different, though. This was the call I'd been waiting for. She finally stood up for herself. She finally told him that she refused to watch him self-destruct anymore. She gave him an ultimatum – rehab and counseling or divorce.

He tried to downplay the situation, but by the time EJ and I finished talking to him he agreed to go to rehab.

Not wanting to waste any time, we drove him to Prolific right away. He was about to back out when he found out that the program would be a year instead of six months, but my mother stood firm and he agreed and checked in.

As soon as we walked out of the clinic she broke down. Had herself a good cry. But by the time we made it back to the house she had a look of peace that I can't recall ever seeing. Me and EJ stayed over for a few hours. Helped her clean up and get rid of the alcohol from all of his hiding places. Then I went to work and tried to get in as many hours as I could.

"Lil bit is on Tinder," Jordan said with amusement in his voice.

It was because of that amusement that I thought he was just playing. Harlem couldn't possibly be on Tinder. The hell would she be on Tinder for? Before things got better between us she was saying she didn't want to date. So what was the point in her being on Tinder? Especially now. I mean... we weren't in a committed relationship but damn. Was she talking to other dudes? And if so... the fuck have I been sitting around being faithful to her ass for?

"You didn't hear me, Tage?"

"I heard you; I just don't believe you."

"Here. Look for yourself."

Jordan handed me his phone and I had to squeeze it to keep from throwing it at the wall.

"The hell is she doing on here?"

"Ima swipe right," before I could even get my threat out he was laughing and lifting his hands in surrender, "I'm just playing. Relax."

After tossing him his phone I pulled mine out of my pocket and stood. Did I have a right to be as mad as I was? We weren't in a relationship, so technically she had the right to talk to other guys and date them. Just because I wasn't talking to anyone else didn't mean she had to follow the same rule.

Nah.

Fuck that.

She *did* have to follow that rule.

After the hard time that she gave me at the party for dancing with someone else she definitely has to follow that rule. She said she wasn't talking to anybody then. So was she lying or was this page new?

My thoughts were all over the place as I dialed her number and waited for her to answer. Really I didn't expect her to, though, because she was at The University of Memphis for registration. With the way I was feeling... if she didn't pick up I was going to pull up.

"Tage... I'm so glad you called. I'm still at registration and Hayden needs dry clothes. One of the kids at daycare spilled their grape juice on him."

"You fucking with other dudes, Harlem?"

A few beats of silence passed before she asked, "What do you mean?"

"I mean are you fucking with other dudes?"

"...No."

"Are you talking to them?"

"Where is this coming from?"

"Are you?"

"No, Tage."

"Then why are you on Tinder?"

Harlem breathed loudly into the phone.

"How do you even know I'm on there?"

"That doesn't matter. Why are you on there?"

"Because... Princess was going on and on about me needing a backup just in case you didn't act right. She said she didn't want me to go back into the state I was in the first time you left, so I needed to have someone lined up that I could talk to to get my mind off you when you left."

Not able to even respond to that foolishness right away, I sat down and scratched my eyebrow.

"You *expect* me to leave? You're planning for that?"

"Tage... can we talk about this later?"

What was the point? My words didn't seem to matter. I'd been repeating ever since I came back that I wouldn't leave. I've been trying to show her with my actions that I'm committed to her and our son, yet she still feels the need to prepare for my exit.

"We don't have to talk about it, Harlem. To be honest I'm tired of saying the same thing over and over again; especially since it doesn't seem like I'm getting through to you."

"I'm not talking to anyone on there. I mean... I made a few matches, but that's it. And it wasn't with the intent to hurt you, Tage. Or to try and replace you."

"I'll um... Ima let you go. I'll take care of Hayden."

"Tage..."

"That's it, Harlem."

I disconnected the call and sat there for a few seconds before heading to Hayden's room to grab him something to wear. Jordan came up to the loft looking sad as hell. Like this was his fault. It wasn't. It wasn't even Harlem's. It was mine.

"I didn't mean for shit to go left like that, bruh, but I couldn't *not* tell you."

"I know, and I appreciate that. We good."

"Aight. Ima go so you can take care of my nephew."

"Aight."

My phone chimed as I went through Hayden's drawers. Figuring it was a text from Harlem, I ignored it. I didn't check my phone until I was in the car, and sure enough it was a text from her.

Angel: I'm sorry. Don't be mad.

You good.

And she was. We just weren't. Not anymore. And I was tired of trying to make us good. I was tired of trying to win a battle for her... against her. She was the only thing, the only person, standing in the way of us. How in the hell are we supposed to overcome that?

HARLEM

"You got me in trouble," I admitted softly as me and Princess flipped through the dresses on the rack.

With her leaving for Nashville soon we were spending a lot more time together than I thought we would this summer. I would be lying if I said I wasn't going to miss her, but we'd kind of gotten used to not being around each other. It probably wouldn't hit us that we were no longer in high school together until we were on campus in our first classes without each other.

For our entire four years of high school we were in the same homeroom class together.

I'd gotten used to seeing my ace's face every morning. That would definitely be the biggest adjustment.

"What I do?" she asked all sweetly.

So sweet it made me roll my eyes.

I couldn't even be mad at her, though. Had I taken my phone from her and not allowed her to make the Tinder profile I wouldn't be in this mess. And even if she did make it I didn't have to keep it or use it. Okay, well, I didn't really use it. So maybe I did. I just like... matched up... but I never messaged them or replied to their messages. That was acceptable, right? I guess not since Tage had been barely speaking to me for the past week.

My baby was tired of my shit. I can't blame him, but he can't blame me either! We're talking about close to three years of guards I had built up. Surely he can't expect them to just crumble after a month or two? Obviously he does.

"Tage found out about my Tinder! Now he's been acting standoffish. His birthday is tomorrow and I don't even know what we're doing because we haven't been talking that much."

Her hands stopped flipping through the dresses as she looked at me.

"What you mean he hasn't been talking to you that much? Is he doing what he did last time? Calling less and less until he stops calling completely?"

"No, Princess. That's the problem. Constantly comparing now to what he did then. I can't blame him for being mad at me. I'm so damn wishy washy it don't make no sense."

"Well, do you really trust him?"

"I do... to a certain extent. It's like... I trust him right now, but what if he starts aviation school and misses football and leaves? What if he thinks he made a mistake? What if when he tells his father he talks him into changing his mind? It's just too much that can go wrong, Princess. I can't enjoy what's going right because I'm worried about what could go wrong."

"You think you're gonna get anything out of here?"

"No."

"Good. Let's go to the food court so we can sit down and talk."

"K."

We walked to the food court in silence, but that silence ended when Princess grabbed my hand and squeezed.

"Girl. Ain't that the same girl from the party a while ago?"

"Who? Where?"

Princess pointed in the direction of Steak Escape. Sitting at a table right in front of the cash register was Tage, Jordan, and their friend Webster. The girl that Tage was dancing with at the party was leaning across their table with a wide smile. Her hand kept gliding over Tage's hair, and every time she did it my eye twitched.

Yea, he was doing that uncomfortable shift that he did when someone besides me or Hayden touched his hair, but still! If his ass didn't want her touching it he should've told her to stop!

I started to not say anything. I started to just walk away and forget I ever saw them. But that shit wasn't working. Before I could stop myself, I was walking over to their table, pushing her gently to the side and asking Tage...

"So this is why I've been hearing from you less? Because you're giving other females my time?"

Tage sat back in his seat. He looked from me to her before chuckling and shaking his head.

"I know she did not just push me out of the way," ole girl asked herself.

"She did, and if you're smart you'll let it go and not try to do anything about it," Princess warned.

Tage stood, grabbed my arm, and led me away from the table. He didn't speak right away, though. He just looked down at me like he wanted to shake me. His jaw clenched as he scratched his eyebrow.

"You're impossible, Harlem."

"I'm impossible?"

"Yea. I don't even know what to say to you."

"Say she isn't the reason I haven't been spending much time with you."

"She isn't."

"Are you lying?"

"Why would you ask me to say the shit if you weren't going to believe me?"

"I want you to say it only if it's true."

"It's true."

"Then I believe you," when he didn't say anything I continued, "Why have things changed, Tage?"

"Because, babe," his hands went to my cheeks. He used them to pull me into his chest, "I feel like I'm sticking around just to watch you burn our bridge. It feels like it doesn't matter what I say or do you don't see what you have in me. You're so blinded by the bad I did that the good doesn't matter to you."

I laughed as I covered his wrists with my hands. That sounded so much like what I was telling Princess just a few minutes ago. It was true, too. Just like I was worried about the wrong that could happen and overlooking the right... I was so focused on the bad that I couldn't appreciate the good.

"I don't mean to make you feel as if I don't appreciate what you're doing, Tage. I do. Things were going good between us. Yea, I have my issues with this... but they're my issues and I've been trying to work them out on my own. I don't want this Tinder thing to make you doubt the fact that I take us seriously just as much as you do."

"Do you?"

"I do. I really do. It's going to take me some time to fully get over that, Tage, but I want to get over it. I *am* going to get over it. Just... I just need a little more time."

"I don't want you talking to nobody else, Harlem. Damn us not being in a committed relationship. You're mine and I'm not trying to share you with nobody but Hayden. You need to deactivate your Tinder and every other account Princess meddling ass set up for you."

Tage hugged me fully, causing a smile to spread across my face.

"She wasn't meddling. She was just looking out for me."

"When it comes down to me she doesn't have to. *I* got you. Never doubt that."

"Okay. I guess I'll let you get back to your... whoever she is to you."

"Don't start that shit. She ain't nobody to me."

"Then why was she touching all on you, Tage?"

"Because she wants me. You know there are women that actually want me, right?"

"Whatever, Tage," I tried to push him away from me, but he held me tighter. "You know I want you."

"Then act like it, woman."

"Okay. Okay."

Tage lifted my head and looked into my eyes.

"You know you're the only one I want, though. There's nothing that she or anyone else can offer me. I only want you."

"I'll take your word for it, but if I *ever* see another woman touching *any* part of you..."

His hands were squeezing my ass.

His lips covered mine.

He kissed me so good... so long... I forgot what I was even talking about when he pulled away.

"Shut that shit up. Always think you running some. You only control what I let you control, Harlem. Remember that. What you and Princess doing here anyway?"

"I need something to wear for your birthday."

Tage pulled his wallet out and handed me three hundred dollar bills.

"Buy something red."

TAGE

"Are you enjoying your birthday so far?" Harlem asked as I merged into traffic.

Hell yea I was enjoying my birthday. It started with her showing up at my apartment and serving me breakfast in bed. Then we went to church with EJ and my mama. After that Charlie and Knight surprisingly took me out to lunch and gave me a nice monetary package.

What was the most fun, though, was going to the park with Hayden and Harlem and flying the model airplane she got me. I could've did that for the rest of the day, but we had to take him back home because she also got me courtside tickets to the Grizzlies game. I planned on watching it anyway because I had a few bets going, but seeing the game live sure beat the hell out of watching it at home on my TV. Even if it was a 50-inch flat screen. As I predicted, the Grizzlies won and I made enough money off my bets to pay my rent up for the rest of my lease.

So yea, I was definitely enjoying my birthday.

"I am. This is the best birthday I've ever had. There's really only one thing that could make it better."

"What's that?"

"If you spend the night with me."

It was dark, but that didn't stop me from being able to see her smile when she looked over at me out of the corner of my eye. As much as I wanted to look over at her I couldn't. Knowing her she was going to say no and I wasn't trying to face her when she did that.

"Okay, but we have to go and get Hayden."

"You'll stay? For real?"

"Yep. Let me call Charlie and see if my daddy has brought the kids back yet. If he hasn't by now he's probably keeping them all night."

She said yes. I couldn't believe it. Not only did she say yes, but she said yes without putting up a fight. If she was always going to be this easy going on my birthday I couldn't wait for the next one!

"Hey, Charlie. The kids back yet?" I looked over at her and could tell Charlie's answer was no by the pout on her face. "Oh. I was gonna come and get DenDen. Tage wants me to spend the night with him," her laugh quickly turned into a groan. "No! I am *not* saying that! If I come home to get some clothes you better not say it either! Knight! Fine!" Harlem put the call on speaker and held her phone between the both of us. "Okay, Knight. I put you on speaker."

"You bet not bring another baby home. And tell Page if he wants you spending the night with him he needs to propose. Ain't gon' be no shacking up 'round here."

"Wow, boo. Is that it?"

"Yea, that's it."

"Now put Charlie back on the phone."

"Oh my God I'm so sorry. Tell Tage I'm *so* sorry."

Charlie was always so sweet and sincere.

"It's cool," I said through my smile.

I'd learned the best way to handle Knight was to just let that mane say whatever he wanted to say and take it with a grain of salt. Wouldn't do me any good to be bothered by it anyway. That wouldn't stop his crazy ass from talking crazy.

"We'll be there in like 15 minutes, Charlie. Please keep Knight in your room until we leave."

"I'll do my very best, sweetheart. Have fun!"

"K thanks."

Harlem disconnected the call and slid her hand under mine. I locked my fingers with hers and kissed her hand. Finally, I'd have her to myself with no distractions. I just hoped she was prepared.

Harlem squinted as she got out of the car and grabbed my hand. When we first pulled up I had her to sit in the car for a few minutes. She thought it was because I had to clean up, but that wasn't entirely true.

Leading her up the stairs had my heart beating fast as hell. I was more nervous now than I was before a big game. I guess it was because there was no way for me to be sure how she was going to react. Yea, she was saying she was invested in this... in us... but there were days when I couldn't help *but* question that.

We stepped into my apartment and her feet stopped moving. Harlem looked up at me with the most fearful look on her face. You'd think I was throwing her to a pack of pit bulls the way she squeezed my hand and stepped backwards towards the door.

"Tage..."

"Gone in."

If the music that was playing had her reacting like this... Lord help. Her steps were hesitant, but she slowly made her way down the hall and into the living room.

"*Tage*," her voice was thick with emotion. She hated crying. Hated being soft and showing her emotions. Her heart. "What did you do?" I didn't answer. Just gave her time to take in the sight before her. The candles. The roses. Her strawberries and cookies. The wine. "But it's *your* birthday."

"I don't know when I'll have you alone again so I wanted to take advantage of this moment."

To be honest, I'd had the candles and shit for a while. Just couldn't snatch the right opportunity. I took a chance getting the strawberries and cookies today, but I knew if all else failed I'd at least have her over for a few hours. Most of the time we spent together was with DenDen, and when we did go out alone I couldn't get her to stay too long because she wanted to be home to tuck Hayden in.

I adored the way she took care of our son, but tonight... tonight I wanted Harlem the woman. Not Harlem the mother. Not Harlem the hurt ex. Not Harlem the businesswoman. I wanted Harlem the woman. *My* woman.

She was standing there with tears flooding her eyes. They started to pour when I walked over to her and put my hand at the small of her back. Harlem turned and wrapped her arms around me. Hugged me tight. Held me close.

"Tage..."

"I love you, angel."

Didn't tell her every day. Didn't want her to think I took those words lightly. Wanted to show her with my actions and consistency that they were true. But I couldn't keep them inside of me in this moment.

I wanted to tell her every time I talked to her. Every time I looked at her. I wanted to shout the shit out in the middle of the street. I wanted to fall to my knees and thank God for second chances every time she looked at me.

I wanted her to be able to trust that. To trust me. I knew Harlem, though. And I knew that this was harder for her than she wanted to admit. Fucked with me tough knowing I'd hurt her so bad for so long, but there wasn't anything I wouldn't do to prove to her that that wasn't me anymore.

Harlem lifted her head from my chest and looked up at me.

"You do?"

My hand gripped her neck softly.

"You know I do, Harlem."

"I love you too."

I resisted the urge to kiss her and led her to the couch. Tonight wasn't about sex to me, although I wanted her bad as hell. It was about getting closer to her emotionally. Mentally. Spiritually. That's the kind of intimacy I wanted to experience with her right now.

Step one – go first.

If I wanted us to be intimate... if I wanted that intimacy... I'd have to see into her and she would have to see into me. We would have to open ourselves up to each other. I would have to open up first and get her to see that she could open up and trust me.

"Can I be honest with you, Harlem?"

Just that question alone had her reaching over and grabbing my hand.

"Always."

"Today could've gone completely different if I didn't have you and Hayden. My birthday has never been something special to me. Most times I'd end up having to play, or my pops would be watching a game, or he'd be drunk and we couldn't go out or have anyone around. It was always something. So for you to have gone through the effort of not only spending the day with me, but getting your family involved as well... that meant more to me than you can understand."

"I kind of understand," she smiled sadly and lowered her head briefly, "After my mom died birthday's weren't really a big deal to me anymore either. Well they were to me, they just weren't to my father. He'd tell me happy birthday and get me a card. That's it. Carmen would send me a card. Most years she forgot to call until the day after. Knight almost always was on the road for my birthday, but he'd have this big arrangement of flowers, balloons, and a cake delivered every year.

I didn't start going out for my birthday until I was like 14 with Princess. Her parents would take us to whatever restaurant we wanted and she'd pay for me," her head lowered again. Her smile lightened up, "It wasn't until I had Hayden that I valued life enough to start celebrating my own birthday and other's birthdays with love and happiness. So I really wanted today to be special for you. It wasn't much but..."

"Are you crazy? It was perfect. You combined everything I love, girl. You and my son. My love for airplanes and sports and betting. How could you have made today any more special, Harlem? You made today everything and I really appreciate you for it."

I don't even think she realized she scooted a little closer to me with a smile.

Step two – desire. We have to be able to fulfill each other's wants and needs. To fulfill we have to know.

"What do you want and need from me, Harlem?"

She pulled her hand from mine and placed both of hers in her lap. While she thought over my question, Harlem ate one of the strawberries. Then a cookie.

"My mommy would always tell me to look for a man like my daddy and Knight. That they both had ways that were good that I needed and ways that were bad that I needed to avoid. I was freaking five and six then so I didn't know why in the hell she was telling me that, but I know why now.

It was because she wouldn't be around to watch me grow older and help me make wise choices when it comes to dating."

"You think dating me was a mistake?"

"No. I think the timing of it was wrong and right at the same time. I think we needed love and acceptance and we got it from each other when we both needed it most, but we just took things a lot faster than we should've."

"So you don't regret carrying my seed?"

"Not at all. Would I have liked for it to happen years later after we were married? Absolutely. But I don't regret Hayden at all. I love that little boy and he is who he is because of the connection and mixture of us. Regretting you would be like regretting the part of him that's you and I would never do that."

Shit. Now I was the one smiling and scooting closer to her.

"But to answer your original question, I need you to be a father to our son. To nurture him in the ways that I can't. To teach him how to be a man. If things were to get really serious between us and we got married, I'd need you to provide for us. Protect us. Lead us. But for now… I just need you to be there for Hayden. And to love me. Make me a priority. You're already taking care of my needs, Tage."

"What do you want from me?"

"I want you to be my best friend again. To spend time with me and give me attention and affection. Make me feel… that weird fuzzy way that only you can. I want you to take control of us and stop letting me deny us of what we both want. What I'm too afraid to have. I want you to not give up on me. Not question how I feel about you. I know I have my moments where I can be difficult, but I don't want you to think I don't want you because I do. I want you to make us work. And I want you to tell me you love me. Every day."

"That's not going to make you run away?"

"No," her cheeks raised and I knew her crazy ass was about to say some slick shit, "I'm not going to say that I'm never going to snap on you again. It certain things you say and do that bring up bad, hurtful memories, but I give you my word that I'm going to try my hardest to not punish you for something that I've already forgiven you for."

"That's fair. I'll give you your time to sort this shit out, but it ain't gon' be no yelling at me five years from now when we on baby number three for what I messed up with baby number one."

Her mouth fell open before she smiled.

"Baby number three? Just how many children do you expect us to have?"

Her smile fell. Head tilted.

"What's wrong?"

"When you left I cursed your seeds and swore I'd never let you put them inside of me again, but as I sit here with you... like... I don't want to have children with anyone else *but* you."

"So that means you're gonna marry me?"

I felt the shift. Something that had been unclicked inside of her clicked. And when it did her energy connected with mine. With what I'd been feeling since I came back. It felt like we were finally getting on the same page. Like she was finally letting me in and accepting that I wasn't here to do anything but stay and love her.

"Yes," she whispered softly. "If you ever asked me to."

Shit was right now a bad time to ask? Ya boy was tempted. We still had a lot of work to do, though. But isn't that what marriage is about? Partnership? Growth? Experiencing life and love with one person until God decided it was over for you on earth. There was no doubt in my mind that me and Harlem... we'd link back up in heaven. I'd recognize my angel there because I was blessed to have her here. I'd recognize her spirit. And she'd recognize her name engraved in the center of my heart. Right along with Hayden's.

"What do you want and need from me, Tage?"

I held my hand out for hers. She placed hers inside of mine.

"I want you. Period. I want you. All of you," her eyelids fluttered. Harlem inhaled deeply. She shook her head. But she didn't pull away. "I need you to trust me. To respect, support, uplift, and love me. I need you to be my place of peace. I need you to marry me. Influence me and make me better. Give me about three more kids. I need you to let me love you for the rest of our lives. Will you let me?"

She chuckled and shook her head again.

"I don't have a choice, Tage. All this time I've been single and saying I didn't want to date. It wasn't because I didn't want to. I just didn't want anyone else but you. I've been saving all my love for you. For *this* you. I don't have a choice but to love and be loved by you."

I had about 18 other steps that we had to go through, but fuck it. There was no way I could not kiss her. Not touch her. Not make love to her.

"Harlem, I really didn't want tonight to be about sex, but I'm reaching my breaking point, angel. I don't know how much more of this I can take before I..."

"Go deep. Fill what you left empty."

HARLEM

"Go deep. Fill what you left empty."

Did I really just say that shit? Knowing good and damn well I said I wasn't going to have sex again until I was married. Did I really just say that shit? I guess I did because Tage took a handful of my hair and used it to pull me to his lips. His kisses were just as slow as they always were, but they were harder. Like he was trying to keep what little control he had left.

I'd lost myself in his lips. His tongue. His hums. And didn't come to until I felt him between my legs. Breaking our kiss only to pull my shirt over my head. Then his lips were right back on mine. Tage's fingers were on the back of my bra working to get it off while his lips went to my neck. With little to no effort he found the spot he introduced me to years ago.

"That's... that's my spot," I warned him.

He didn't stop.

Tage licked and sucked harder. Making my body shiver and warm as he finally unsnapped my bra. He tossed it across the room. Lowered his lips down my chest. To my breasts. Taking them into his hands one at a time. Circling around my nipple with his tongue until it hardened. Then he'd lick it. Take it into his teeth so gently I could barely feel it. Close his mouth around it and have me squirming underneath him.

His hands...

God I...

I can't understand how my hands never fit intertwined with another man's hands...

But Tage...

Tage's hands fit mine perfectly.

They fit me perfectly.

Every part of my body they touched he branded. Reclaimed. And when he made his way between my thighs...

He took his time.

Placed a slow trail of kisses down my stomach.

Ignoring the impatient open and close of my legs. My thighs. Wrapped around his head.

Why was he making me wait?

His fingers began to pull my leggings down. I expected him to remove them quickly. To act how I felt. Like a child that's been teased with presents under the Christmas tree. This was Christmas. It was time to finally unwrap our presents. I expected him to rip me apart. To show me the yearning he'd been trying to stifle since the day I slammed the door in his face.

But Tage took his time.

Unwrapped me like he wanted to savor every second of the gift I was giving him.

Allowed his eyes to roam every inch of my body as he undressed me.

No part of me was left untouched. If not by his hands, or his mouth... he touched me with his eyes.

"Are you sure?"

His voice was strong and calm yet shaky. Like that control... that control was slipping even more. I found that to be true when instead of waiting for my answer Tage positioned my legs around his shoulders and sent his tongue from the bottom of my entrance to the top of my clit.

Licking up the cream that puddled up at my center.

Moaning as he swallowed.

His hands went to my thighs and he pulled them apart.

"Are you sure, Har–"

"Ye–."

I hadn't even gotten it out before he was latching onto my clit, and I truly did not mind. Just as quickly as he pulled it into his mouth is as quickly as he released it. His tongue swirled around my clit. Between my lips. Down to my entrance. And he was sucking my clit into his mouth again.

His hands gripped my waist. Slid up my stomach. Squeezed my breasts. Our eyes connected. He smiled.

Smiled.

Looked me in my eyes as he consumed my pussy with his mouth. Licking until I arched off the couch. Sucking until I trembled. Blowing until I relaxed. Just to start over again and make me climax.

I didn't mean to push his face away so hard, but the shit felt so good and came so strong I couldn't control it. Tage chuckled as he stood and undressed.

"Sorry," I mumbled breathlessly.

Covering my face, I tried to regulate my breathing and prepare for what was next. Even at 15 I knew Tage was blessed between his legs. Before I gave him my virginity I let that crazy Princess talk me into watching a few videos to see what I'd be in for. Because Tage was just a year older than me I figured there was no way his dick would be the size of the men in the videos I watched. There was no way he'd have me moaning and yelling like the women in the videos I watched. No way would he make that cream come from inside of me like the women in the videos I watched.

I was wrong.

Tage was blessed.

I remember looking at it the first time thinking… the hell am I supposed to do with that? How is that supposed to fit inside of me? But it did. Perfectly.

Tage took my wrists into his hands and pulled mine down from my face. My eyes started at his. Traveled down his chest. His eight pack. And that V that was the perfect guide for what was between his thighs. It was a little longer. A little thicker. Still had the same veins. Same darkened tip. Some days it would be long and straight. Some days it would be long and curved.

Today… it was curved.

"Harlem," I returned my attention to his face. His knees rested against the couch. He wrapped my legs around his waist. "You know that… I adore you. Right?"

Before I could answer he was pushing himself inside of me. Slowly. Inch by inch. Filling me. Deeply. Doing just what I'd asked him to do. Taking away the emptiness. My hands went to his shoulders. Nails dug. Legs squeezed. Breath hitched. Back arched. Mouth opened. His closed. His hummed. Right in my neck. Right by my ear. I could've came just like that. *Just like that.*

Tage wrapped his arms around me and lifted me into the air. Kissing me and my neck as he carried me into his bedroom. He placed me on the bed and pulled himself out of me. I watched as he went over to his dresser and grabbed a condom from his top drawer.

"I really don't want to wear this," he admitted walking back over to me, "But I don't want to get you pregnant again and Knight kills me."

"Smart man," I teased as he made his way between my legs.

"I wanna see every face you make," he said under his breath, spreading my legs... pushing my knees into the bed... and pressing his way back into me. "I wanna see you cum on my dick."

If he didn't shut up it would be happening a lot sooner than I wanted it to. I really didn't have much of a choice, though. Not with him stroking me so slowly. So deeply. Had my lips trembling. Mouth moaning. Eyes closing. Walls clenching. Heating. His hand went to my neck. The other to my waist. Still stroking just as slow. Just as deep. But harder. And longer. So long he was pulling all of himself out, just to slide right back in.

Lips trembling. Mouth moaning. Eyes squeezing. Nails digging. Breath hitching. Walls clenching. Walls flooding. Walls pulsing. Legs shaking. Back arching. Him humming. Me coming. Him stopping. Me coming. Him kissing me. Moaning into my lips how much he loves me. Me... too jaded to say it back. Him patient. Him waiting. Me... opening my eyes and finding love in his. In him.

"I love you, Tage."

"Then marry me."

Tage wrapped one of my legs around his waist and hooked the other one at his elbow. Face to face. Chest to chest. He was fucking me down. Literally. Brushing his pelvis against my clit so precisely I came back to back. Even harder this time. His lips were on mine. He ate my moans until they turned into whimpers and heavy breathing.

"Marry me, Harlem. Will you marry me?"

How did he expect me to think... to answer... with him digging so slow and so deep and so hard his entire bed was shaking? I was shaking. Struggling to breathe, but gahhdammm this would've been a nice way to die.

His hands were at my face, trying to get me to focus. I wrapped both legs around him tightly. Pulling at his hair. Moaning and cursing. Cursing and moaning.

"Harlem..."

"Yes!" I cried out, coming again.

He stopped, but I didn't. I couldn't. He waited. Until my orgasm was over.

"Yes to marrying me... or was that a yes to how good this dick had you feeling?"

With a chuckle, I lifted myself to peck his lips.

"Both, Tage."

"You'll marry me? Harlem, don't play with me..."

"I'm not. I will. I love you, Tage. Of course I'll marry you. I love you."

I caressed his cheek as he processed my answer. Out of nowhere we both started laughing. Tage lowered himself to kiss me and I happily accepted as he began to move inside of me again. This was my dude. My biggest freaking headache. My best friend. My love. My all.

"Damn, Tage. Can you cum already?"

"Girl, please. I ain't had you in years. We going all night."

TAGE

Waking up with Harlem next to me made me feel like I was dreaming. Was this real? Were we finally getting our shit together? Did I really propose? And she said yes? I didn't want to ask about it because I didn't want her to change her mind. There was really nothing stopping us but time. Why wait?

I loved everything about this girl. From the way she snored lightly and held onto me for dear life as she slept. To the way I had to convince her to get up and get her day started every time we woke up together. From the way she squinted and rolled her eyes to the way she cried and got physical when she was upset. Don't even get me started on watching her get dressed. I could watch Harlem put on her panties and shimmy into her jeans all damn day.

The thought of this being my life had me smiling as she walked over to me and kissed me. Only thing missing was Hayden, and that was about to change when we went to pick him up.

"Tage?"

Her fingers brushed my cheeks. My neck. My hair.

"What's up?"

"Did you mean it?"

"Mean what?"

Her head lowered. Almost in shame. I lifted it by her chin and kissed her.

"I meant it, angel. Did *you* mean it?"

She smiled and bit down on her lip with a nod.

"Yes. I meant it."

"Good," I smacked her ass and stood. She followed me into the kitchen. "I'll get you a ring. And give you a dope ass proposal we can tell our family about. Unless you're cool with..."

"No, Tage. When people ask me how you asked me to marry you I don't want to say while we were having sex."

"Why not? What's a better time to talk about becoming one than while we are one?"

Harlem smiled and shook her head as she opened the refrigerator. I don't know why. Wasn't anything in there.

"Really, Tage? How do you live, bruh? What do you feed my baby when he's here?"

"We eat out. A lot."

"Obviously. Ain't nothing in here but waters, two lunchables, and some yogurt."

"Pass me a water while you're in there."

She did with a roll of her eyes.

"We're going grocery shopping today. You at least should have some fruit and vegetables in the house, Tage."

"That's what I need you for."

"Whatever. And after we pick DenDen up you're getting a cooking lesson."

"Mane, Ion wanna learn. I got some noodles in the pantry and it's plenty of restaurants around here."

Harlem ignored me and shook her head again as she left the kitchen.

This wasn't the life I thought I'd be living at 20, but it was damn near perfect. Only thing that would make it perfect was having my family living with me. Hayden's little short ass had one of those smaller baskets and was walking around the grocery store picking out his own groceries.

When I told him that he could pick whatever he wanted to stock up the apartment you would've thought I told him I was taking him to meet SpongeBob or some shit. And so far he was doing very good. Most of his basket was filled with fruit and vegetables and healthy snacks, which made me even more grateful for Harlem because she was obviously bringing him up right.

He had a few things in there that weren't healthy like ice cream, cookies, and airheads, but who could blame him? His mama had a sweet tooth out of this world.

"Tage, what kind of meat do you want?" Harlem asked. When I didn't answer her right away she looked at me, "Chicken and what else? Fish? Beef will be easy for you."

She was really pushing this me learning how to cook thing. I mean… I knew how to cook certain things. Like eggs. I could cook eggs. And noodles. And I could make a fire can of tuna or chicken salad. All that other shit was going to have to be reserved for her. I had absolutely no interest in learning how to cook. Especially after what happened with the blackened catfish.

"No fish," she must've thought about it too because she started cracking up. "That shit wasn't funny, Harlem."

"Yes it was. I'm so sorry but it was hilarious. I wish you could've saw your face, Tage. You were so sad and disappointed."

"I told you I wanted it to be special for you."

"It was. It really was. It might not have been the romantic special you were hoping for, but it was special, and I will never forget that," she started laughing again, "Like ever. In life."

"Alright. Aight. Just pick some shit so we can go."

HARLEM

"So listen, I was hoping that maybe... we could not mention the whole engagement thing while you're here."

Knight was barbecuing for the fourth of July and surprisingly he invited Tage before I could even invite him. It was weird. Them being all... nice to each other. But I was glad about it. A month had passed since Tage's birthday and the whole marry me thing and so far we'd done a pretty good job at hiding it.

Okay, well, I was hiding it. Tage was just the kind of private person that didn't tell anyone his business. It wasn't that I didn't want to marry him or want people to know that we were getting married... it's just that... it happened so fast, you know? I went from hating him to being engaged to him in like... a month. But that's how things had always been between us. Fast. Abnormal. I don't know, though.

I guess I was enjoying how things were and I didn't want them to change right away. The look on his face told me he felt otherwise.

"Why not?"

I looked behind me to make sure Knight or Charlie weren't near the backdoor.

"Things are getting better now between you and Knight. I don't want him to think we're rushing. Him and my daddy already think I have too much on my plate and that it's going to be even worse when I start school next month. I just don't want to ruin the progress we're all making. It's been hard enough for us to get past everything as well as we have. And although Knight is being cordial with you... I just don't want to rush it. Can we wait just a little while longer?"

"But I'd be more than willing to help you with your load, angel. That's what I'm here for. All you would have to focus on is being a wife, a mother, and school. I'll take care of everything else. You wouldn't even have to work. Hell, you don't have to now. Just hire some more people."

"Tage, you know I don't like people."

"No. You don't like being left by people. Hurt by people. Disappointed by people. But you gotta let that shit go, babe. You have to get some help."

He was right. I only had three employees because I didn't like depending on a lot of people. Having only three kept not only the drama down, but the disappointment down as well. I did need help, though.

"I'll consider it. But can we keep this between us for now. Please?"

"I feel like you're doing this because you still don't trust me to stick around."

"Tage..."

"But I said I'd prove it to you so it's whatever. That's fine, Harlem."

"You mad at me?"

"Nah," fell from his lips, but his eyes said yes.

I took his hand into mine and led him to the backyard.

"Charlie's having a girl. Guess what they're going to name her?"

He looked down at me with lighter eyes.

"What?"

"Harlie."

"Harlie? Like..."

"Charlie but with an H like Harlem."

His smile matched mine.

"Aww that's sweet, babe. That's really sweet. I'm sure y'all are going to spoil her rotten."

"You already know."

"Daddy!"

Hayden dropped his toy and ran towards us and I found myself smiling again. I'd been doing that a lot lately.

"What's up, baby boy? You helping your uncle grill?"

"Hell naw," Knight answered, "But you can."

I made my over to Charlie as Tage went back into the house to wash his hands.

"I see it," she whispered, nudging my shoulder softly.

"See what?"

"There's something different between you two. Has been since his birthday."

I looked from her to Knight before shaking my head.

"Charlie, I have no idea what you're talking about."

"Stop lying. Just like you saw that there was something different about me and Knight after the gala… I see something different between you and Tage. Spill it."

"Fine. We had sex."

"Chile please I already knew that. It's something *else*."

Tage opened and closed the backdoor. He looked over at me and smiled as he walked over to the grill.

"Okay. You have to promise not to say anything, Charlie. You can't say anything," she made the gesture of sealing her lips and I laughed at her silly ass, "That night… Tage asked me to marry him."

One of her hands flew to her mouth while the other seized my wrist.

"Did you," she covered her mouth again, "You did," she covered her mouth again, "Did you…"

"Charlie!" I whisper screamed as I gripped her face. "Stop smiling so damn hard. You know Knight picks up on things."

"Oh my God. Oh my God. Oh my God. I'm so excited!"

"*Charlie*!!"

She covered her face, squealing and laughing hysterically. Knight and Tage looked over at us and I shrugged feigning innocence.

"Charlie, I ain't telling you *nothing* else!"

"I'm sorry. Let me get myself together. Let's go inside."

She grabbed my hand and pulled me up, only to stop and look at Tage. Her arms extended for an air hug, and both Tage and Knight looked at her like she was crazy. I pushed her arms down, keeping the right one in my hand, and pulled her into the house.

"Charlie," I paced back and forth as she wiggled and danced, "You have to keep this between us."

"Why? Why don't you want anyone to know? Or is it just Knight that you don't want to know?"

That stopped my pacing.

"I can't believe I'm saying this out loud…"

"But…"

"With everything happening so fast I'm just... I don't want to rush into this foolishly. I love him and I want this... I just don't want to be disappointed if it doesn't happen. If he leaves. He says he isn't but I'm just not sure. It won't be as hard and embarrassing if the engagement falls through and no one else knows about it."

"Oh, baby, come sit down," we sat next to each other and Charlie took my hand into hers. "Is he not doing something that you need to feel secure?"

"That's just it, Charlie. He's doing everything right. He's being active and present and that's honestly all I ever wanted. He's made me and Hayden his priority. Just as sweet as he's always been. It almost... feels... too unreal. Like this is all a dream. Like I'm going to wake up and he still be in Alabama. It just... I can't believe that he's back and he's so... right."

"That's understandable. Sometimes we find ourselves blessed with things, people, relationships... that seem too good to be true. You feel as if you don't deserve those things. And you end up sabotaging them because you don't believe they're real. You don't believe they're yours. That you deserve it.

Let me ask you this... are you willing to lose him to prove that this isn't real? Because I can look at him and tell that he means this, Harlem. If you sabotage this out of fear... you might get what you're trying to avoid. Him leaving. Is that what you want?"

"Of course not."

"Then, sweetheart, let it go. Enjoy this second chance you have to live the life you want with him. If he's taking care of his business the rest is up to you. It's up to you to believe and trust. Don't mess it up."

"You're right. Thanks, Charlie."

She smiled and kissed my cheek before standing and going back outside. Was it really that simple? Why did it seem so hard?

TAGE

As far as my pops knew, I was in Alabama resting up from a sprained ankle. That's why I couldn't tell him anything about summer practices. That's why I wasn't participating in the scrimmage. That's why I couldn't tell him if I was going to get the coveted first quarterback seat on the roster.

I was tired of lying.

Tired of avoiding his phone calls because I didn't want him to ask me 50 questions about school, football, the team, and Alabama.

There was no way I could keep this lie up for an entire schoolyear, so I decided to go and visit him. He wouldn't be expecting to see me on a weekday and that was made apparent by the look on his face as I walked over to him. He'd been in rehab for about two months and we were already seeing the old him resurfacing.

The him that wasn't angry and abusive.

To be honest, the real him had become a stranger over the years.

I was glad to have him back, though.

He stood and we hugged before sitting across from each other.

"What are you doing here, Tage? Shouldn't you be on campus? And why isn't your ankle wrapped up?"

I chewed on my top lip for a few seconds before answering.

"I... I withdrew, Pops."

His arms crossed over his chest as he leaned back in his seat.

"You withdrew?"

"Yea. I moved back to Memphis this summer. Started working at Downtown Aviation. That's... that's where I'll be going for school this year."

He scratched his eyebrow, showing me where I got it from.

"Why, Tage? I thought football was your dream? The best place for you to be is Alabama."

"Football is *your* dream, Pops. Not mine. Never has been. Never will be. I've never wanted to play professionally. That was all you."

"Why didn't you say anything?"

"I did," I yelled louder than I wanted to, "You never listened, or you just didn't care."

He cupped his hands together and placed them on his forehead.

"I'm sorry, son. I didn't realize... I couldn't realize... I'm sorry. I wanted a better life for you than I had. I won't apologize for that, but I will apologize for trying to force you to do something you didn't want to do."

I didn't realize how much I needed to hear that until he said it. And before I could stop my eyes they were watering.

"I wanted to please you and make you proud, but I had to come home and live my life for me. For my son. He's the most important thing to me. Him and Harlem. I wasn't sure how you would take this. I just had to let you know."

"I respect you for standing up for what you want and what you believe in. I can't imagine how hard this must have been for you over the years. My father used to terrorize me emotionally and mentally and I swore I wouldn't do that to you and EJ, but I screwed you up in other ways."

"It's... fine. It's not fine, but I'm good. I'm home. I got my family. You're getting better. It's cool. I know you weren't really yourself when you were drinking. Just continue to get better. Get back to yourself. Maybe we can play a game or two when you get out of here."

"I'd like that, son. I'd like that very much."

HARLEM

On days neither of us had class, Tage and I had date night. With Everett Sr. being gone Patricia was taking full advantage of having the house to herself. When she wasn't working she had Hayden and I couldn't be happier. Without my mommy, Patricia was the only grandmother he was going to have. I wanted nothing more than for them to work on their bond.

Most times we went to a game, comedy show, or the movies and grabbed something to eat, but tonight Tage was up to something. Instead of him picking me up he told me to meet him at his place. As soon as I got into my car there was a card taped to my steering wheel that read –

You've put up with my bullshit over the years. I deeply regret being the cause of your fears and tears. But now I'm committed to making you smile. Head to the place we conceived our child.

That little booger.

I squealed as I dialed his number and of course he didn't answer. Anxiously I made my way to EJ's house. The night Hayden was conceived EJ was out of town on a business trip, so Tage spent the night over there. I'm sure I don't need to tell you what happened next.

The entire ride to EJ's house I thought over what the hell Tage could be up to. What could be the last piece of this hunt? This puzzle. What did he have in store for me? It couldn't have been any better than the sheer excitement I was feeling right now, though.

I made it to EJ's place in record time. When I knocked on the door EJ handed me a bouquet of roses with another card attached to it that read –

I will admit when you first gave me the news of me being a father it gave me the blues. My reaction was one that you weren't expecting because I couldn't see that our son was a blessing. My eyes have been opened to his worth and yours. Your next clue will be behind the guest bedroom door.

"Tage, what are you up to?" I asked while walking past EJ into his house.

My hand shook as I opened the bedroom door. Laying in the middle of the bed was the huge teddy bear Tage gave me for my 15th birthday. Around its neck was a heart shaped necklace. I slept with that bear every night. Wore that necklace every day. Until I told him about the baby and he pushed me away. When he did I stopped by his house and put them both on his doorstep.

After taking the necklace from around the bears neck and putting it on mine, I hugged the bear. Squeezed it. Took in its scent. It smelled just like him. The clue had completely slipped my mind at the sight of the bear. Had it not been taped to the door I would've left and forgot all about it.

I want you to have back all that truly belongs to you. That includes me and all of my love for you. Your last clue is at my apartment and EJ has the key. You'll find it where I asked you to marry me.

"EJ!" I yelled, then jumped when I saw him standing in the hallway outside the door. He handed me the key with a smile. "Thanks."

"No problem. Have fun."

"I'm already having fun."

I was halfway down the hall when his voice stopped me.

"Harlem?"

"Yea?"

"He really loves you. Don't ever doubt that."

My hand went to the necklace absently and I clutched it.

"I know he does, EJ. I know."

But was love really enough? Was love all that mattered? It had to be. I needed it to be. I needed it to release me from all the other feelings that were consuming me.

So I get to his apartment, and his living room is empty. Completely empty. All of his furniture is gone. No pictures on the wall. Nothing. The kitchen was empty too. The hell? Was this some sick joke? Was this his way of leaving me again? I knew he'd gone to visit his father; was he changing his mind about us?

"No."

He couldn't have taken me through all of this just to leave me. My back rested against the wall as I dialed his number. This time he answered.

"Hey."

"Tage? What the hell is going on? Where are you?"

"Where are you?"

"In your apartment. It's empty. Are you leaving me?"

"Did you do what I told you to do?"

"Well, no, but..."

"Go into the bedroom for the last clue, Harlem. I'll see you in a few."

Tage hung up and I groaned loudly as I forced my feet to move. His bedroom was empty too. There was a card in the middle of the floor where his bed used to be.

I got this apartment when I was alone. But it will not suffice for our starting home. We need more room for Hayden and our new babies. Turn around and introduce yourself to our realtor – Mercedes.

Turn around and introduce myself to our realtor Mercedes?

I read the last line twice before turning around and jumping at the sight of a woman with her shoes in her hands.

"Goodness, lady. You scared the *shit* out of me."

She laughed and walked over to me as I clutched my chest.

"I'm sorry. I was in the hallway closet waiting for you to read the note. I'm Mercedes. It's nice to meet you, Harlem."

"You as well. What does he mean our realtor? You mean to tell me he moved and bought us a house?"

Mercedes shrugged as she stepped into her shoes.

"I'm going to let him go over that with you. I'm just here to lead the way to him."

Well, I'd played along up until this point. Might as well keep it up. We walked outside. Mercedes got into the car that was ironically parked next to mine. Funny. I hadn't even noticed it before. Guess I was too focused on getting inside and finding the next clue.

Mercedes pulled out and I trailed her to a neighborhood that was in the Cordova area. Instead of pulling into the driveway Mercedes parked on the street. We met between our cars and she handed me a key.

"What is this?"

She pointed to the house we were parked in front of with a smile.

"Tage is my baby cousin and he has taken more initiative to secure his future with you than my own husband did and he's twice Tage's age. You better hold on to my cousin, Harlem."

Mercedes hugged me, but I couldn't even hug her back. I was too caught up on her words. Secure his future with me? Was this… no. He couldn't have.

"Go on," Mercedes urged.

Small steps led me up the driveway. Up the porch. To the door. Trembling fingers struggled to hold the key steady as I pushed it into the lock. Lungs inhaled air deeply. Eyes sealed shut. This had to be a dream. This would be when I'd wake up. When I would open my eyes, in my bed, and realize that this had all been a dream.

There's no way this could be my life.

Not after everything I'd gone through.

Who was I to finally get a happy ending?

People didn't get these.

That was a fairytale.

And my life had been nothing like a fairytale.

But when I opened my eyes… I was still here. Still standing at the door of this house with my hand on the knob. Was this real?

I opened the door and stepped inside.

"Tage?"

He didn't answer me. After locking up behind myself I walked through the house. When you first step in there was a set of stairs that led to a bonus room. There was a huge living room with a fireplace and large window. It gave the perfect view to the backyard. The living, dining room, and kitchen had hardwood flooring. Behind the kitchen was the laundry area and pantry.

A long hallway led to two bedrooms on the left. A bathroom in the center. And another room on the right. Every door was opened except for the room on the right, so I figured that's where Tage was.

I wondered if he felt me? If he knew I was there? If he knew that I was too afraid to open the door? But I did, and when I did my knees gave out of me. Acting fast, Tage caught me and kept me from hitting the ground.

"What's wrong, angel? Have you eaten anything today?"

In the center of the master bedroom he had a pallet with my favorites. Candles lined the room along with rose petals. There was no music this time. Probably to keep me from coming directly to this room when I first got here.

"You did all of this for me?"

"I did all of this for us," Tage wiped my tears and continued as I tried to find the strength to stand on my own, "Mercedes hooked us up. Blessed us with a lease to purchase. I wasn't sure if you'd like it as much as I did, so we're just going to rent it for now. If you want us to buy it we can," I opened my mouth to speak but nothing would come out, "I put my furniture in storage for now. Figured we could pick some shit out for the house together. This is yours... ours... whenever you're ready. Whenever you're ready to get married and start our lives together. This will be our home."

"Tage..." my words... still escaped me. I jumped into his arms and he laughed and held me tightly. "I don't know what to say."

"Do you like it?"

"I fucking love it! It's beautiful! Can we really afford this?"

"Yep. You know I was paying a stack for my apartment. This is eleven hundred."

"That's it?"

"Yep."

"Tage. I... I love you so much. I'm really just... thank you."

"You don't have to thank me for this, Harlem. This is what I'm supposed to do. You and my son belong with me. I'm willing to do whatever it takes to make that happen."

There was no way for me to express with words just how happy and full he made me in this moment. I removed myself from his body and fell to my knees.

"Harlem... what are you doing?" he asked as I unzipped his pants.

"About to let you feel how much I love you."

TAGE

"You were serious?"

No, was *she* serious?

Here we are... on top of Skyview Terrace. Just the fucking two of us. I reserved this shit because I wanted tonight to be special. Not only was it her last night before starting college, but I wanted to propose in a more traditional way. A way that we could tell our families about. So I rented the place out and had the top of the roof decked with food, drinks, music, candles... nice shit.

Now when I proposed to her a little over two months ago she asked that we keep the engagement between us for then. Something about giving Knight and her father time to see that they could trust me with her and that we weren't rushing into things. That was cool. I respected that. I understood the fact that things were moving pretty fast between us. But they always had. Harlem and I... nothing about us was normal. Nothing about us was slow. But I gave her that.

Now I'm on top of this roof, on bended knee, ring in hand, looking like a damn fool. Was this shit a joke to her? The fuck?

"The fuck you mean was I serious, Harlem? Hell yea I was serious. Why would I play about some shit like marrying you? I got us a fucking house! A house that I've been staying in by my damn self because I've been waiting on you."

I stood and got all up in her personal space. Normally I'd try to be nice and patient and understanding but I was tired of her shit. Harlem took a step back and ran shaking fingers through her hair.

"I just... I thought you were... I mean I know you were serious, but a ring? That's... that's *serious*."

"So that's what this is about? You don't mind us being engaged, you just don't want anybody to know? You don't want this ring to have people questioning you about us?"

Harlem rubbed her ring finger absently.

"It's not that I don't want them to know. I just don't want them to know right *now*. I need time, Tage."

"The fuck do you need time for? I'm sick of you hollering about time. Time ain't gon' heal those wounds. Time does not heal wounds, Harlem. If it did we wouldn't be in this position for some shit that I did three damn years ago, girl. If time was going to heal those wounds they'd be healed, angel.

The only thing that time does is numb you of the pain. And that shit doesn't even last for long because eventually you're going to be forced to deal with the shit. Those wounds are going to be reopened and worse than they were before. And that's *exactly* what's happening now. Time is our enemy. The longer you push us off the harder it's going to be for you to commit to me.

The only thing that's going to heal those wounds is God and letting me fix what I messed up by loving you. What's so hard about that shit? God I don't..." I took a step away from her and covered my face as my head shook. "I don't know what else to do, Harlem. I swear I don't know what else to do. I'm trying to do right by you. I don't know what else to do."

"Tage, I'm... I said yes. I want to marry you. I want to be with you. I don't understand why you're making such a big deal out of this. What difference does it make if we tell people or not? If I wear the ring or not?"

My voice was calmer than I felt on the inside as I said, "It's not about them, Harlem. It's about you. It's about you trusting me and having faith in me. It's about you committing to me and allowing me to be the man that you need."

After placing the ring back in my pocket I closed the space between us.

"Listen, I love you. I know I fucked up, but I love you. I love you so much that I'm willing to put my feelings and desires aside to give you what you need. I wanted us to get married now because that was our goal, right? So what difference would it have made if we got married now or seven years from now? With you starting school and wanting to move out I figured this time of transition was perfect. We could move in together. Take care of Hayden together. Make this thing work. As a family. But you're obviously not ready for that."

"So what? *Now* you're going to leave?"

"No. I'm not. I'm just going to fall back and give you the time and space you think you need. We can still talk and go out and shit, but marriage… that's off the table. I *refuse* to let you make me feel bad about the boy I was then. I'm a man today. And this man deserves the same amount of love and respect that he's willing to give you. When you're ready for Tage the man he's yours. But you gotta let go of Tage the boy first, Harlem. Damn."

Her eyes watered. She turned to the side so I wouldn't see. I wanted her to tell me that I was right. That she was tired of playing around and she was going to get her shit together. That she wanted to marry me and wear my ring proudly as a symbol of our love. Our union. But instead of saying any of that she said…

"You're right, Tage. You deserve that. You deserve better than what my fear and paranoia is allowing me to give you. It's always fine when we're just hanging out, but when things get serious I get scared. That's not your issue it's mine. I need to figure out how to deal with that. Until I do… maybe we should just… focus on Hayden instead of us."

"You know what, Harlem? Fine."

HARLEM

Fine.

He said fine.

Fine.

That was the last thing Tage said to me a few weeks ago. All of our communication has been done via text since then, and it's always about Hayden.

What did I expect?

I couldn't blame him for not putting up a fight.

What the hell is wrong with me?

He was offering me everything I wanted everything I needed and my crazy ass pushed it and him away.

My issues... they ran deep. This wasn't about Tage and it wasn't fair of me to make him suffer because of it. What can I say? I was tired of people leaving me. Tired of people saying they loved me all while choosing to be away from me. Hurting me. I was tired of that shit!

First it started with my mother.

Gone.

Then it was my father.

He was alive, but he was dead emotionally. I was in that house alone after my mommy died. All he did was take care of my necessities and nurse his broken heart. It took me having Hayden and him wanting to be a better grandfather than he was a father for him to see just how fucked up he treated me after she died.

Then it was Carmen.

Left.

Ain't came back yet.

Swears she loves me but don't give a damn about what's going on in me or her nephew's life. Hell, Knight either! Maybe she loves us, but she's so wrapped up in her own little life that she's just completely walked out of ours.

Then it was Knight.

He was already on the road playing basketball before mommy died, but when she died he really stopped coming around because of his guilt. Had it not been for me getting pregnant he would probably still be living the same loveless emotionless lifestyle. He'd still be fucking different women running from commitment. But thanks be to God that he allowed Charlie to give him a love he could feel.

He left, but he returned.

And Tage.

They say the ones you love the most have the power to hurt you the most. It didn't matter how young I was when we met, I fell in love with Tage the moment I heard his voice. Saw his face. Felt his heart. I've tried and tried to downplay my love and feelings to make it hurt less, but the fact that I went through such extremes just made my love for him clear even more.

And for years... not days... not weeks... not months... but years... years went by and day after day I struggled with loving a guy that seemed to have no love for me.

He left, but he returned.

He returned and was the same but so different.

More active.

More mature.

Wiser.

Better.

But every time I looked in his eyes I was reminded of every time I was left.

"Excuse me, do you mind if I take this chair?"

I looked at the wide smiled girl whose hand was already clutching the chair. Her smile reminded me of Charlie. People like them seemed to have this natural cheerfulness about them. Before I met Charlie I thought it was because their lives were perfect and they hadn't gone through anything before, but she showed me that wasn't true. She went through hell and somehow found a way to be happy and love and live free.

"No, take it."

I needed to talk to Charlie. I need to know how she found the courage to shake off all that she'd gone through and chose to love and live. I need to know how she allowed herself to trust Knight and give him a chance after the last man tainted her. How she became brave enough to put her heart on the line without a guarantee that it would be love that was returned instead of pain. I need to know... and soon... before Tage left for real. For good. Not because he wanted to, but because I pushed him away.

The sight of Tage's car outside caught me off guard. He was supposed to be at school, not at my house. I took my time going inside because I honestly wasn't prepared to talk to him. It didn't matter, though. He wasn't inside. Tage was out in the backyard flying the little blue model airplane he'd gotten Hayden.

The sight made me feel worse. He was doing so much, trying so hard, and... ugh.

"He adores the both of you."

Jumping at the sound of Charlie's voice, I turned to face her. Her usual bubbly smile was softer and more empathetic than anything.

"Yea, he's great. Can I talk to you before I go to work?"

"Absolutely."

"Okay. Let me go speak to my baby and I'll be right back."

The sound of the door opening caused Hayden and Tage to look at me. Hayden smiled widely, dropped the remote to the plane they were flying, and ran towards me. Tage's thumbs went into the elastic of his sweatpants as he stood there and watched me lower to Hayden's level.

"Hey, baby!"

"Hey, Mommy!"

I kissed his cheeks and squeezed him until he fell into a fit of laughter. When he was done I released him and stood.

"Were you good today?"

"Yes, ma'am. I was good!"

"Good. Have you eaten anything yet?"

"Daddy got me some Chick-fil-a after daycare."

"Okay. Well, Mommy has to go to the store in a little while, but I'll be home in time enough to fix you something to eat and get you ready for bed, okay?"

His lip poked out at the same time his eyes watered.

"Do you have to go?"

"Yes, but I'll be back before you miss me. I promise."

"But I miss you already, so you *can't* leave."

Balancing Hayden, work, and school was a lot harder than I thought it would be. The great part about it was all of my classes were in the morning, so while he was at daycare I was at school. Only thing was, now when I wasn't at the store I was having to do homework. I wasn't able to give him as much time as I could before. We weren't able to watch cartoons or read or play for hours before it was time for him to go to bed.

"I'll make you a deal; if you are a big boy when it's time for me to leave I'll bring my work home. That way I can do it here and you can be with me while I do it. What about that?"

Hayden nodded and opened his arms for another hug. I happily gave him one. Tage walked over to us, but his eyes were on Hayden.

"I'm about to head out, young man. I'll see you later, okay?"

"Okay, Daddy."

"You don't have to leave, Tage. I won't be here long anyway."

"It's cool," he mumbled, still avoiding my eyes.

Tage gave Hayden a hug and tried to go back in the house, but I grabbed his wrist to stop him. Funny. Now I see how he felt when I couldn't look at him.

"You didn't give mommy her kiss, Daddy."

"I was letting her save them for you," Tage answered.

"We share. We're each other's remember?"

My grip around his wrist dropped as I opened the door and ran up the stairs. I didn't want Hayden to see me cry, and I definitely didn't want Tage to know that I was feeling bad about how things were between us. Not now. Not yet. Not when it was hard for me to understand what was going on with me fully and how to fix it.

I didn't want to play with him and lead him on. I didn't want to go back to him until I was ready and able to give him what he needed from me. And had a tear dropped from my eye in front of Tage he would've comforted me. That comfort while I was vulnerable would've led to me being in my feelings and trying to get back to the way things were. Then we'd end up right back here.

By the time I was done getting myself together in the bathroom Charlie was standing on the other side of it.

"Wanna talk about it?" she asked.

"Is he still here?"

"He left."

"Okay. Where's…"

"Hayden's downstairs playing with KJ."

I nodded and followed her into my room. She sat at the edge of my bed while I crawled up to the top of it. As I slid under my comforter and covers I asked her…

"How were you able to let Knight in? What did you do to be brave enough to try again after what that guy did to you?"

Charlie was 19 when she had her heart transplant. After she got my mommy's heart she had a permanent reminder – a scar going down the center of her chest. Some asshole made her feel bad about it and she shut down. Started wearing nothing but button down shirts and shirts that came up to her neck.

As beautiful as she was, Charlie was insecure.

She hadn't dated a guy after that for 10 years.

Until she met Knight.

Now she never wore button down shirts.

Now you couldn't pay her to cover up her scar in shame.

"Honestly, Harlem, I didn't do anything. If I did anything it was letting Knight in. He's the reason I'm as confident and comfortable in my skin as I am today. He literally loved the pain out of me. I just... let him love me. Nothing special."

My face must've expressed how I felt on the inside because Charlie giggled.

"That's it? That's all you got for me?"

"Yep," she shrugged and tickled my foot as best as she could, "It sounds simple, and in theory it is... but if it was as simple as you make it sound we wouldn't be having this conversation. You'd be letting Tage love the pain out of you. But you're not."

Damn.

That was true.

It *wasn't* easy.

People always talk about how hard it can be to love after you've been hurt... but they hardly ever talk about how hard it is to let someone love *you* after you've been hurt.

"So you're telling me all I have to do is let Tage love me? Just... accept his love and let things flow as they will and everything will work out?"

"That's exactly what I'm saying. When you've been hurt, left, rejected... it's natural to put your guards up. You did what a lot of women don't know how to do – you put yourself first. You protected your own heart and made sure no man could hurt it or you again. But, sweetheart, the sucky thing is... when you close the door to pain you also close the door on love.

The key is to find the balance in protecting your heart through wisdom but keeping it open for love. You have to choose to let people in that would never do anything to intentionally hurt you. People who would hurt themselves before they hurt you.

You want me to give you some advice that's concrete... just... fuck it. Say fuck it. Say fuck it, Harlem. Say it. Say it."

"Okay!" I yelled through my smile. "Fuck it."

"Say it like you mean it. Say fuck it!"

"Fuck it! Fuck it! Fuck it!"

We both laughed, but that shit kind of made me feel a whole lot lighter. A *whole* lot lighter.

"Just say fuck it, Harlem. Just let it go. Take a chance, baby. Be realistic. You know there's a chance that Tage can hurt you, but there's also a chance that he won't. Be mindful of what can happen either way. Embrace your fear. Then live. Live in the moment. Love in the moment. In this moment. Today. Fuck it.

Fuck the past. It doesn't exist anymore. You're suffering and punishing him and yourself for something that no longer exists. Fuck the future. It doesn't exist yet. You're worrying yourself over what Tage may or may not do during a time that doesn't exist. The past is no more. The future is not yet. All you have is now. And right now… Tage is here. He's present. And he loves you. So what are you gonna do about it, Harlem?"

"Fuck it. Ima go and get my man back."

TAGE

Seeing Harlem break down like that did something to me. It was one thing for me to think that this wasn't effecting her... but to see her cry, well try to hide the fact that she was crying, that shit messed with me. It reminded me of the night I proposed. When I asked her what she wanted and needed from me she told me not to give up on her. Not to give up on us. To fight for us.

I will admit... I gave up for a while. But seeing those tears in her eyes... those tears in her eyes were real. She's hurting. She's scared. This isn't the time for me to pull away. This is the time for me to love on her even harder.

And that's what I planned on doing.

I called EJ's girlfriend, Reyna, and asked her to come over. She has a timeshare in Miami that I wanted to talk to her about renting. If I could get Harlem and Hayden to go away with me during her fall break, maybe we could at least get back to a place of peace and friendship because right now we weren't talking at all. I could barely look at her ass without getting pissed. Then we'd build on that friendship like we always did. But this wasn't over for us. Not by a long shot.

Reyna called and told me she was outside, so I got up to open the door for her.

"Hey, Tage."

"Hey, what's up? Thanks for stopping by."

I hugged her and caught sight of Harlem's car parked on the street. She was standing on the side of it looking at me. Watching me hug Reyna. Probably thinking the worst about me right now. What was she even doing here?

Since Harlem made no effort to come to the door I told Reyna to make herself comfortable and that I'd be right back. The closer I got to Harlem the closer she got to her car. She didn't get inside, though. Her arms were crossed over her chest as she leaned against her door.

"Hey, everything alright?" I asked when I stood in front of her.

Her eyes shifted from mine to the door.

"Um, yea. Everything's fine. Sorry for just stopping by without calling first but I didn't think you'd answer."

This wasn't my Harlem. No spazzing. No attitude. No trying to put her hands on me. No trying to go upstairs to question Reyna. She was behaving for a change. Wow. But she wasn't fooling me. Her eyes kept going up to the door. She wanted me to explain having another woman in the house. In *our* house.

"It's cool. What's up, though?"

"Um..." her arms dropped to her sides. She looked up at the door again as she scratched her cheek. "It can wait. Why don't you just call me after your... company leaves."

Now that got a chuckle out of me. I could have easily told her that Reyna was EJ's girlfriend, but I didn't. She deserved to sweat a little for playing with my emotions. I'd tell her later tonight after Reyna left and I had the plans together.

"You sure, Harlem? What I got going on with her can wait if you need to talk, babe."

Harlem smiled as she took ahold of my shirt. She used it to pull me into her. I pushed her into the car gently and watched as she bit down on her lip.

"It can wait," her smile... her confidence... "We have all the time in the world to talk."

"Is that right?"

Her smile widened.

"Right. Just call me."

This girl. She wouldn't have been so mad and hurt if she didn't love me first. She loved me. First. Above all.

"I will most definitely call you, Harlem. Most definitely."

"Okay."

She pushed me away and got into her car. I waited until she was gone before I went back into the house.

"Was that her?" Reyna asked as soon as I sat down.

"Yep. That's the wife."

"Why didn't she come in? I want to meet her."

"You'll meet her soon. We got some things we need to work out. That's actually why I wanted to rap with you. I wanna rent your spot in Miami for a few days."

"Rent? Boy, bye. Just let me know when you want to go and go. You don't have to pay me anything."

"You sure, Rey? I really want to pay you. I know that's your side hustle."

"If you want to pay me just work out those things you need to work out and give EJ some more nieces and nephews so he can stop asking me for kids."

"Girl, you better give my brother some kids."

"Whatever. Ain't no babies coming out of *this* vagina."

I laughed at her silly ass as she pulled her phone out and showed me some pictures of where I'd be taking the family soon.

HARLEM

He didn't call.

All last night. All this morning. All this afternoon I'd been thinking about the fact that he didn't call.

Tage thought he was slick. I'm sure he thought he was making me jealous, but I knew that was Reyna. I'd never met her personally, but there's pictures of her all over EJ's home. I used to see them all the time when I took DenDen over there or picked him up.

I let him have that, though.

But he didn't call.

Why didn't he call?

A million reasons floated around my mind and none of them relieved me. Was he really tired of waiting for me? Playing with me? Had I finally pushed him away?

I wanted to stop by his place after I picked Hayden up, but I was unaware of the protocol for shit like this. Like was I supposed to let him come to me? I didn't want to seem like I was pressing him, but since we weren't talking because of me was I supposed to be the one that fixed it this time?

Lawd.

I'll be glad when we finally get it together.

That's the funny thing about it all.

As fearful as I am of losing him... I still can't see myself with anyone else. Ever. I know I know I'm young. Yea, I have the rest of my life ahead of me. But Tage... Tage soothes my soul. That's not something I'm willing to let go of.

"What do you want for dinner, baby? I don't have to go to work tonight."

"Yay! I want chicken nuggets!"

I looked at Hayden through the rearview mirror and chuckled.

"I said I'm cooking. I ain't cooking no chicken nuggets. We might as well go to a drive-thru for that."

"Well... okay... what about a cheeseburger?"

"Hayden..."

"Milkshake!"

"That ain't no food! You're just calling out random stuff, silly!"

"Chicken nuggets!"

"What about chicken tacos?"

He twisted his face up and squinted his eyes while thinking my suggestion over.

"Okay. Are we eating it at daddy's house? At the new house?"

"Um... you don't want to eat at our house?"

I looked at him in time enough to see him shrug and lower his head.

"I just wanted us to eat it with daddy. He likes them too."

"I don't know, Hayden. Daddy has work and class today so I'm not sure. I'll check and see, though, okay?"

Hayden nodded and scooted down in his seat. As usual we sang every song we knew that came on until we pulled up to the house. After getting him out of his seat, I texted Tage as we walked to the house.

Tacos tonight?

To keep myself from checking my phone every few seconds I put it in my purse and tried to forget I'd even sent the text.

Knight was on the road and Charlie was supposed to be at work, so I was surprised to hear water running in the kitchen. Hayden wasted no time climbing the stairs up to his room while I went into the kitchen to see who was home.

It was Charlie.

"Hey, Charlie. What are you doing home so early?"

She put the electric tea kettle that she was filling up on its base before turning to face me.

"Where's Hayden?"

Her voice. Her eyes. Something was wrong.

"He's... in his room. What's wrong, Charlie?"

"I'm not sure."

"You're not sure?"

"There was an accident."

"An accident? What kind of accident?"

Charlie licked her lips and rubbed her hands together as she walked over to me.

"They don't have all the details yet, but it was on the news. Something about one of the student planes at Downtown Aviation. Something about a blade losing power and the plane crashing. They aren't saying who was involved…"

"Plane crashing? Plane crashing? Plane crashing?"

Charlie grabbed my shoulders and stared into my watering eyes.

"Relax, Harlem. We don't know that Tage was involved. Have you talked to him recently?"

"No," I sobbed trying to pull myself away from her. "I haven't talked to him since yesterday! I need to get to the school!"

"I'll drive you."

"No, please. Stay here and watch Hayden. I don't want him there if…"

I started crying and shaking even harder. The words couldn't even fall from my mouth.

"You don't need to drive, sweetheart. You're shaking like a leaf in the wind. I'll take Hayden next door and drive you. Here," Charlie took my hand and sat me down at the table. "Wait right here while I take the boys next door."

My elbows went to my thighs. My hands went through my hair. This couldn't be happening. Tage couldn't have been on that plane. He couldn't die. He couldn't leave me. Not like this. Not permanently. We had too much to do. Too much of the world to see. Too much love to experience. To make. And I'm running around wasting time because of fear.

No more.

No fucking more.

I refuse to let fear rob me of another second of life.

It's no way to live.

No way to live.

"I promise," I prayed as I fell to my knees, "God, I promise. Just let him be okay and we'll do this right in Your eyes. We'll get married and do right by You. Raise Hayden up on Your word and do right by You. Just please… please don't take someone else that I love away from me."

"Okay, Harlem. Let's go," Charlie's hand wrapped around my arm and she helped me stand. "Don't worry yourself sick, sweetheart. We don't know anything yet."

"But what if he was… what if it was him, Charlie? What am I going to do?"

"We're not even going to go there. We're not going to talk about that. We're not even going to accept that as a possibility."

With each step I took my legs felt weaker and weaker. I took my phone out of my purse and checked to see if Tage had texted me back. He hadn't. I called. He didn't answer.

This could not be happening right now.

This cannot be how it ends.

TAGE

"Harlem is headstrong. She's unyielding. Man, once she gets stuck on something, it's hard as hell to get her to change her mind. Just continue to fall back and give her the time and space to realize how much she loves, wants, and misses you. Let some time go by of you just coming around for Hayden. Let her see what she has in you. She'll come around then."

Knight's words... that was the only thing that kept me from calling Harlem last night. Had I not talked to him after Reyna left I would've called her. I couldn't let too much time pass, though. The fact that she showed up yesterday said a lot. That was big for her.

I decided to go and see her tonight after class, but with one of our planes crashing things have just been crazy today. Thankfully Huey and his teacher weren't hurt. They had on parachutes and were able to jump before the plane crashed. Between all of the parents and family members that were showing up and the newscasters, paramedics, fire trucks, police cars, and ambulances the entire street was damn near blocked off.

My instructor came and told us that was it for the day and if we could get out of the parking lot we could leave, so I was about to head out when I heard my name being yelled. It sounded like Harlem, but there was no reason for her to be here. I turned towards the direction it sounded like the voice came from and saw Harlem running towards me. *Running.* Tears were streaming down her face as she ran.

I jogged towards her fearing something was wrong with Hayden, and the second I was within reach she fell into my arms and held me tightly.

"What's wrong, angel? Is something wrong with Hayden?"

When she didn't answer me I peeled her off my chest to look into her eyes.

"Harlem…" her hands stroked my face as she continued to cry. "Harlem, talk to me. What's wrong?"

"I… I thought it was you. On the plane. I thought you were on the plane that crashed."

She made her way back into my chest and I held her close. Just that quickly I'd forgotten all about the crash. It didn't register in my mind that she was worried about me; my only concern was her and Hayden.

"Why didn't you answer your phone?!" she pushed me away from her and punched the shit out of my chest before hugging me again. "I called you! I texted you! Why didn't you answer the damn phone?!"

"It's in my car, Harlem. It's in the car. I'm so sorry you were worried about me, but I'm fine. I'm fine."

Harlem let me hold her for a few seconds more before she pushed me away again. Charlie came walking over to us as quickly as she could.

"Glad to see you're okay, Tage," Charlie said as she hugged me. "I'll be in the car, Harlem."

"That's alright, Charlie. You can go on home. I got her."

"You sure?"

I looked at Harlem as she wiped her face.

"I'm positive. Thank you."

She waited until Charlie was gone before she asked, "Why didn't you call me yesterday?"

"Your brother told me not to."

"What? Since when do you listen to Knight?"

"I listen to him with all things Harlem and Hayden. He felt like I should give you space so you could make your way back to me on your own."

She lowered her head and mumbled, "I don't want any more space."

I lifted her head by her chin and Harlem closed her eyes as more tears fell.

"What are you saying, Harlem?"

Opening her eyes, she inhaled deeply and took my hands into hers.

"I'm saying I love you and I'm tired of living in fear. I'm tired of waiting for something to happen that may never happen. I'm tired of being in pain because of the past and worrying about the future. I'm saying I want us to be together. I want us to be a family.

The entire ride here I just kept thinking about how if I lost you... these past few days... I'd have nothing really to remember you by. To remember us by. And that hurt worse than anything. I know we won't live forever, but I want us to spend the time we do have together. Making memories. So when things are over for us..."

"Only through death."

Harlem smiled as I pulled her into my chest.

"When one of us dies... the time that we will have spent together will carry the other one through. Instead of focusing on us being apart for whatever reason... I just want to focus on us being together and in love."

I took her cheeks into my hands and kissed her forehead. Her nose. Her lips. Her cheeks.

"Are you sure, Harlem? I'm not playing this back and forth game with you. If you're not ready for this..."

"I am ready. I promise I'm ready, Tage. I love you. You said that's all that matters. I know that now. I believe that now. I love you."

I'd be a hypocrite if I gave her a hard time. If I allowed fear to keep me from trusting her. From going all in. I had to take the lead and show her what trust really looked like.

"Okay, Harlem. If you say you're ready... I trust you. I love you too."

She smiled with half of her mouth before telling me to, "Prove it."

"How?"

Harlem looked around at all of the people that were around us. All in their own conversations and worlds.

"Ask me again."

"Ask you again?"

"To marry you. Ask me again. I mean... if you still... if you still want that. With me."

This girl.

"I don't know what I'm going to do with you, Harlem. You are something else."

"Love me. That's what you can do. Love me."

I kissed her twice softly as I pulled the ring out of my pocket. When she saw it she smiled and covered her mouth with her hands. After taking the ring out I pulled her hands down and kept the left one in mine.

"You've carried it around with you, Tage?"

"Yea. Been waiting on you."

Her eyes watered again as I kneeled.

Something felt different this time. It was heavier. Like this time it meant more. I closed my eyes and took in two full lungs of air before opening them and speaking.

"Harlem, I love you. I've been in love with you since the first day I laid eyes on you. You've been my friend. My lover. My supporter. The mother of my child. The only thing left is for you to be my partner in life. For life. As my wife," her hand went to my cheek and she caressed it with her thumb. "Will you marry me, angel?"

She nodded and jumped into my arms so hard I almost fell.

"Yes, Tage. Yes. Yes. Yes."

Her lips were all over my face. Covering it with kisses as those that took notice of what was going on applauded. When she'd had her fill of me she held her hand in front of me and allowed me to slide the ring onto her finger. Harlem lifted her hand and looked from me to the ring.

"I love you so much, Tage. Thank you for not giving up on me."

"I let you go once and that was the biggest mistake of my life. I'm *never* doing that again."

>KNIGHT<

"I just want Knight," Harlem whined from inside of the room that held the ladies of her bridal party.

Four months after Tage proposed for what I found out was the second time they were getting married. He surprised me. He made up in his mind that he wanted his family and fought for them. Fought *Harlem* for them. That gained a lot of my respect. I wasn't willing to hand my sister over to him until I was sure he deserved her. He did.

I walked into the room and Harlem cried harder at the sight of me.

"Y'all gotta leave," I said pointing to the door. "Charlie, get these folks out of here."

She nodded and ushered Patricia, Princess, and a few of our cousins out as I took Harlem into my arms. Charlie could go into labor with our baby girl at any second so I was already on edge. I didn't need nobody saying or doing anything to make me pop off.

"What's wrong, sweetheart? Are you having second thoughts about getting married?" I asked as I wiped her face.

"No. I'm really excited, boo. I just... Carmen isn't here yet and I miss mommy. I wish she was here with me for this."

"Fuck Carmen. You don't need her. You got me and Charlie. You got Pops. You got her brother Rodney. Her sister. You got EJ. You got his girl. You got Patricia. Hell, even Everett is out there behaving like he got some sense. I know you want Carmen here, but do *not* let her absence ruin this day for you. You got Hayden. And mama *is* here with you. She's here."

I tapped her heart and she smiled.

She had more people supporting her and rooting for her than she realized. The most surprising was Everett. Outside of his brief time away for the wedding, he was still in rehab. Everett was putting forth the effort with Tage and Hayden. He even asked Harlem to start visiting him so he could get to know her better. As of now we all were unsure of what the future held for him and Patricia because she wanted a divorce, but he didn't seem to want to let her go. He was trying to convince her that the abuse was over because his drinking was. I guess she had reached her breaking point with him. We'll see, though.

"Sometimes I feel like I can feel her. You know... like I feel God. But I haven't felt her yet today. I guess that's why I'm a little on edge. But you're right. You're right."

"You sure about this, Harlem? You don't have to marry him today."

"No. I do. I love him, Knight. More than I've wanted to admit. I've been so scared, but I'm not living in fear anymore. I deserve love and happiness. I deserve my happy ending. And I know that it's with Tage."

"Okay, but if he doesn't do right by you..."

"You'll kill him. I know."

Her smile was wider this time around and that made me feel a little more at ease. I let the women come back in, but I stayed in there with her. She wanted me to walk her down the aisle anyway. Hayden and our pops would be in front of us. My baby wanted me at her side, though.

Her makeup had to be reapplied, then it was time for us to line up.

I wrapped her arm over mine and inhaled deeply as I looked down at her. Harlem was my pride and joy. None of us expected her to be pregnant at 16, but she made the best of it. She became a damn good mother, and there was no doubt about it... even at 19... she was going to make a damn good wife.

That was just her nature. Her spirit. She was mature. She was loving. She was hard, but *so* soft hearted. She was smart. Wise. She was ready. I had to be ready to let go.

The music started up and I swallowed, pushing back tears. We started walking and Harlem grabbed my arm tighter and looked up at me with a smile.

"I feel her, Knight. I feel her."

I hugged her and kissed her cheek.

"Good, sweetheart. Good."

We continued down the aisle and my eyes landed on Tage. He was looking at Harlem like she was... *every* fucking thing. Like a man *should* look at his woman when she's making her way to him to become his wife. Being with Tage left Harlem in ruins. Hayden made those ruins beautiful, but Tage ruined her. She loved him still. She saved her love for him unknowingly. And being loved by Tage... being loved by Tage pulled her out of the wreckage.

THE END.

CPSIA information can be obtained
at www.ICGtesting.com
Printed in the USA
LVOW10s2131100417
530296LV00015B/794/P